"Excuse me, I was just leaving the house."

For a long second or two she thought he wasn't going to move. In a dire need to get away, she pushed through the narrow space he'd left her, miscalculated and felt her breasts brush against his shirt as she tried to pass him.

Steve straightened a little too late. Triss stumbled over his foot, and his hands closed about her upper arms.

For a moment they stood together in the stone doorway, bodies touching, Steve's chin only an inch from her temple. She could hear—even feel—the harsh intake of breath, smell clean clothing and soap and a faint, frightening seductive male skin-scent.

In irrational panic she clenched her fists and raised them, thumping his chest. "Let me go!"

He swung her to the outside of the doorway with easy strength, then released her, saying, "Glad to, but are you sure that's what you want?"

Laurey Bright has held a number of different jobs, but has never wanted to be anything but a writer. She lives in New Zealand, where she creates the stories of contemporary people in love that have won her a following all over the world. Visit her at her website, www.laureybright.com

WITH HIS KISS

BY
LAUREY BRIGHT

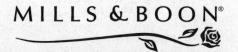

MILLS & BOON®

*All the characters in this book have no existence outside the imagination
of the author, and have no relation whatsoever to anyone bearing the
same name or names. They are not even distantly inspired by any
individual known or unknown to the author, and all the incidents are
pure invention.*

*First published in Great Britain 2004
Harlequin Mills & Boon Limited,
Eton House, 18-24 Paradise Road, Richmond, Surrey TW9 1SR*

© Daphne Clair De Jong 2003

ISBN 0 263 83840 4

*Set in Times Roman 10½ on 12 pt.
02-0704-44036*

*Printed and bound in Spain
by Litografía Rosés, S.A., Barcelona*

Chapter One

Steve knew the moment Triss Allardyce saw him, across her husband's grave as the coffin was lowered into the earth.

The glazed look disappeared from her clear blue eyes that held no hint of tears, and they widened with shock.

Steve felt a savage kick of satisfaction. One black brow rose a fraction in involuntary acknowledgment, and a muscle in his tightly clenched jaw twitched a corner of his mouth into a grim semblance of a half smile.

Triss made a tiny movement, as though she would have recoiled but for the somber-faced, very young men standing close on either side of her, and the crowd of people pressing about them. Then she wrenched her gaze from Steve and turned to take a single white rose from another teenager proffering a basket of flowers.

Shining, pale-honey hair fell forward and hid her face when she stepped up to cast the flower into the

grave. Other mourners filed past while she stood
nearby, accepting their kisses and handshakes and mur-
murs of sympathy.

Steve stooped for a handful of earth. Prettifying the
ceremony with flowers didn't make Magnus's death
any easier for those who had loved and respected him.
Those like Steve and the boys—for they weren't much
more—now gathered protectively about the supposedly
grieving widow.

She'd sat in the front row of the church straight-
backed and perfectly still while a hulking adolescent
beside her sobbed into his hands. Following the coffin
out afterward, she had remained pale and composed
and apparently unmoved even when one of the youngsters accompanying her burst into a Maori karakia, the
lament sending a shiver up Steve's spine with its
haunting passion and forcing him to swallow hard on
a suddenly obstructed throat.

At the graveside she'd appeared more bored than
stricken with sorrow, a faraway look in her eyes as
though her mind was otherwise occupied.

Steve was tempted to skip the drinks and food offered after the funeral but Magnus's lawyer who had
phoned him in Los Angeles to give him the news, had
seemed anxious to ensure Steve's presence, saying they
needed a private meeting.

"At the funeral?" Steve had queried.

"Mrs. Allardyce has agreed we can use one of the
rooms at Kurakaha House. She'd like to get the business out of the way."

She'd like to get *him* out of the way, Steve figured.
Magnus must have mentioned him in his will.

He hoped Magnus had protected the House and its

work from his wife's—widow's—money-grubbing hands.

Beautiful hands, he had to admit when she extended one to him as he entered the big, carpeted double room, already filled with mourners engaged in muted chatter. As beautiful as the rest of her, which had changed little during the six years since he'd seen her last. She'd cut her hair shorter, just below chin level, and maybe lost a little weight, or possibly the clinging black sheath that she wore without adornment falsely lent that impression.

"I'm glad you came, Steve." Her voice was as cool as the smooth fingers he held briefly in his.

Liar, he thought, biting back a sardonic laugh. She'd have been happy never to have laid eyes on him again.

Her gaze didn't quite meet his, focusing instead on the knot of his maroon tie. "Magnus would appreciate your being here. Nigel told you he needs to talk?"

"He told me. I believe you've made a room available."

"Yes." She was distracted by someone at his elbow leaning across to touch her arm. "Excuse me."

Steve was sure it was with relief that she turned to the newcomer. Dismissed, he helped himself to a drink from a nearby table and looked about for the lawyer.

Half a dozen teenagers circulated with trays of finger foods. Residents at the house, no doubt, whom Triss had pressed into service rather than paying caterers.

Cheap. Presumably the food had been prepared in the Kurakaha kitchen, too. The cook had outdone himself. Or perhaps these days it was a her. Not a young and attractive her, though. Triss wouldn't stand the competition.

"Steve?" A burly dark man of about his own age

grasped his arm with a large brown hand. "Steve, you sonofa— You come all the way over from America?"

"I flew in last night," Steve said. "Late. How are you, Zed?"

"Blooming," the big man beamed. "Still working the gardens here, doing a bit of carpentry and stuff. Got a wife and kids now. Two of 'em. Kids, I mean. How 'bout you? Never heard much after you left."

"No wife, no kids."

"Yeah, that's the way." The man punched his arm. "Fancy-free, eh? Got yourself some big house and car in Los Angeles, eh?"

"An apartment," Steve said. "And yeah, I own a car. Don't you?"

"Ford Falcon." Zed grinned. "Beat-up old bomb. Bet yours is better." But his envy wasn't real, and when his wife joined them with one child in her arms and another clinging shyly to her skirt, Zed glowed with pride as he introduced them, swinging the older one into his arms and planting a smacking kiss on her cheek.

"This is a bugger though," he added, sobering as he looked about them. "Old Magnus going like that."

Steve could only agree. "I suppose you don't know what's going to happen to the House?"

"I guess Triss will carry on."

"You think so?"

"She's been holding the place together since Magnus got sick."

Protecting her investment?

Maybe she'd changed. Give the woman the benefit of the doubt, Steve admonished himself. You could be wrong about her being the Wicked Witch of the West. Maybe. He said, "I didn't know Magnus was ill."

"He didn't want people to know."

People? Steve felt a strange, angry pain in his chest. *I'm not "people." Someone should have told me.*

She should have told him. The pain became a burning resentment. He looked across the room at Triss. She was talking to a handsome gray-haired man who looked vaguely familiar. After a moment Steve placed him—a seasoned and prominent politician, a cabinet minister when Steve had left the country. He was holding one of Triss's elegant pale hands in both of his, and she was smiling at him, making no attempt to draw away, listening intently to what he had to say.

Steve's narrowed stare shifted when a former resident of Kurakaha clapped his shoulder and shook his hand, demanding to know what he'd been doing since he'd left New Zealand. Others followed, and half an hour or more passed in social chat.

Mourners had overflowed into the garden. Steve walked through the French doors thrown open to the long tiled terrace, keeping an eye out for the lawyer.

Old oaks and an ancient, spreading puriri shaded the terrace. Looking across the lawn and the native evergreens edging it, he glimpsed the curved, poplar-lined drive, and remembered the first time he'd seen the two-storied, sprawling white building from the gateway. Magnus had stopped the car there, letting the engine idle, and turned to the sullen teenager that Steve was then, saying, "This is your new home."

In spite of himself Steve had been impressed by the size of the place and its air of well-preserved colonial gentility. Magnus, in his way, was impressive, too. Tall, erect and already gray-haired and perilously close to unkempt, he had been an odd mixture of artist, idealist and pragmatist.

The young Steve remained suspicious and surly for months. Until it dawned on him that Magnus wasn't really interested in reforming him. All he cared about was rescuing the raw talent that he'd somehow discerned in this unpromising fifteen-year-old.

Fourteen years ago. And now Magnus was gone.

Steve turned to survey the room behind him, and caught sight of Nigel Fairbrother, the lawyer, just inside the French doors.

"Wait a while," Nigel said when Steve accosted him. "Triss wants to make sure she's spoken to everyone first."

"I thought it was just you and me."

"Best if you're both there together," Nigel said. "No hurry, though."

After the crowd thinned, Nigel caught up with him again and twitched at his sleeve. "We're down here."

Triss was waiting for them in what used to be called the bookroom toward the rear of the house. Besides shelves of books there were rows of video tapes and CDs, and a large TV screen and video player occupied one corner.

She was standing before the window with her hands loosely clasped, the low afternoon sun shimmering on her hair. As Nigel shut the door she sat down on one of the chairs grouped about a heavy, round kauri table, her back rigid.

The lawyer gestured to Steve to sit near her and placed himself opposite, taking charge. Steve left one chair empty between him and Triss.

Nigel dug inside his jacket and pulled out a long envelope. "This isn't exactly a reading of the will," he said, "but—" he glanced from Steve to Triss

"—I don't know if either of you know how Magnus…um…disposed of his affairs."

Triss seemed to pale. She must be anxious about her inheritance.

Steve gave a faint shrug. "No idea."

"I've made two copies so you can both peruse it at your leisure, but essentially, the bulk of his personal estate has been left to his wife, with—ah—conditions attached to some of it." Nigel nodded toward her. "A portfolio of stocks and shares and investment monies is reserved to maintain Kurakaha in its present form as an educative facility for disadvantaged young men, to be administered as a trust—"

Steve gave a silent sigh of relief, relaxing against his chair back, only to straighten abruptly as the lawyer continued "—by the two of you jointly."

"What?" Steve snapped.

"The two of…*us?*" Triss had definitely whitened, her eyes darkening as the pupils enlarged. For a second Steve thought she might be going to faint. Then two smudges of color scorched her cheekbones. "When did Magnus make that will? There must be another one!"

"I'm afraid not." Nigel looked down at the pages as if checking the date. "He never lodged another with us."

"But…he had plenty of time." Triss leaned forward, frowning. "Let me see that."

Nigel handed it over and passed another copy to Steve, who scanned his quickly before looking up.

Triss looked up, too, the tight set of her mouth failing to disguise its lush femininity. "You drew this up?" she asked Nigel.

"At his request, of course. If you have questions…"

"No questions. It's very clear. Insultingly clear. And watertight, I suppose."

Nigel looked unhappy. "I pointed out to Magnus that if he made the whole of his bequest to you dependent on your continuing to live at Kurakaha—because that was his first thought—you might have grounds for contesting. As it stands now he has adequately provided for his widow, although if you leave the House there will be considerably less than if you stay. The actual monetary value of the bequest may have altered over the years, but his accountant will fill you in on that."

"I know exactly what my husband was worth, thank you." There was a brittle note in her voice.

I'll just bet you do, Steve thought. And she hadn't expected that he'd attach strings to her enjoying what he'd left her.

She held the papers so tightly the edges were crushed. Steve realized that her hand was trembling. Perhaps coming to the same realization, she placed the papers on the table, smoothing them out. She hadn't looked at Steve. "We'll have to come to some arrangement." Her voice was unsteady, too, he noted. She paused, and said more strongly, "I don't suppose Steve will be moving back to New Zealand, so I hope he won't feel the need to interfere with—"

"Interfere?" Steve cut across her.

She opened her mouth, then paused again, apparently aware of a tactical error. "There's no need for you to become involved," she said carefully, still not looking at him directly, "just because Magnus never got around to updating his will."

"I am involved. This—" Steve lifted his copy of

the document "—makes us joint trustees. I can't say I was expecting it, but I won't let Magnus down."

With a flare of temper Triss said, "Do you think *I* will?"

Their eyes met, and he wondered how a woman who looked all peaches and cream could have such a steely blue stare. Not that his iron-gray one was probably much different.

Nigel intervened. "I think Magnus believed the two of you had complementary talents and strengths. That's why he wanted both of you—"

"He didn't want it!" Triss argued, returning her attention to him. "He just never got around to changing his will. He was always so busy, but he *must* have meant to. And you—" she rounded on Steve "—you know that!"

"As you said," Steve pointed out, "he had plenty of time. And he's not here to explain. I intend to take my responsibility seriously."

"An absentee trustee?" she scorned.

"Don't jump to conclusions," Steve advised her curtly. He hadn't had time yet to give thought to the implications of this. "And don't think you can get away with anything just because I'm not breathing down your neck every minute of the day."

He knew he'd scored a hit when her eyes flashed blue fire at him for an instant before she let her lids briefly fall. Then she looked up again, her face once more a composed, icily perfect mask. "Naturally I'll consult you over any really important decisions—and I would hope that you'll be reasonable and not veto my suggestions out of hand."

"Now why," Steve asked her, hiding his own anger

under a deceptive gentleness, ''would I want to do that?''

Her look told him she wasn't fooled, but Nigel took the question at face value. ''I'm sure both of you have the best interests of the House and its aims at heart.''

''Are you?'' Succumbing to temptation, Steve knew that Triss hadn't missed the mockery in his voice.

Rather than responding, she picked up the papers she'd placed on the table and rose gracefully to her feet. ''I must get back to my guests,'' she said. ''Thank you, Nigel.'' Reluctantly turning to Steve, she added, ''I suppose we should talk before you leave again for the States. Give me a call in a day or two.''

Without allowing him time to reply she made for the door. Steve got there just before her and paused for a moment with his hand on the knob while she waited, stiff with impatience.

He wasn't a man who usually gave women a bad time, but this one had always got under his skin, and her brusque order to call her nettled him. Yielding to a desire to bring her down a peg, he swept a measuring glance over her, scouting the enemy, silently inspecting the admittedly stunning feminine outline of her figure while making it clear he wasn't impressed.

His reward was an infinitesimal lifting of her chin, even as her answering glance told him he was despicable.

The trouble was, after he'd pulled open the door and allowed her to sweep past him, he was inclined to share her opinion.

Not that it made any difference to his opinion of *her,* he reflected hours later, nursing his third whiskey in the bar of his Auckland hotel, almost an hour's drive north from Kurakaha. Triss had been furious at having to share the trusteeship. There must be a lot of money tied up in the trust and he was damned sure she'd been hoping to milk it for all it was worth, if she couldn't break it.

Maybe Magnus hadn't been dazzled clean out of his mind after all. He seemed to have retained a grain of common sense—enough to not quite trust his wife to carry on his work without someone to keep an eye on her.

Steve was that someone and, although it had certainly surprised him, he didn't mean to take the old man's wishes lightly.

A smile touched Steve's firmly etched mouth. Always larger than life, with the charisma of true genius, Magnus had been a brilliant, world-respected conductor until the early onset of arthritis curtailed his career. As the crippling condition progressed he'd devoted increasing amounts of his time to giving talented but socially disadvantaged young musicians the chance to excel, while filling in other gaps in their education. Taking no more than thirty-five students at a time, for periods of up to four years, Magnus had spared no expense.

Until Triss had come along with her penny-pinching attitude to the House and its work. Steve recalled her apparently gentle nagging about budgets and cost overruns. And Magnus's quiet teasing at her unnecessary concern. Born to a privileged background, his father descended from successful early settlers, Magnus had inherited wealth and had earned large sums from a short but dazzling international career, and as he said, he had no family to spend it on, only Kurakaha and its inhabitants.

Steve had been the first to arrive. Despite clashes between him and his mentor over Steve's plan to make a fortune manufacturing specialized keyboards and sound equipment rather than pursue a musical career of his own, the younger man appreciated the tremendous influence Magnus had exercised on his life.

Steve phoned Triss two days later. She suggested he might come to Kurakaha at ten-thirty. "If that suits you?" she added.

An afterthought.

"Perfectly," he replied, deciding not to be difficult for the sake of it.

"I'll be expecting you, then," she said, crisp as a newly ironed shirt collar. She had put down the receiver before he could reply.

Damn the woman. No one else could tempt him to petty revenge. Firmly he put aside the thought of being half an hour late.

It was a minute before ten-thirty when he rang the bell at the main entry, and Triss herself opened the door to him. This time he kept his gaze firmly fixed on her face, but even so he was aware that the open lapels of her cream blouse revealed a faint shadow between her breasts, and that the silk fabric was tucked into a narrow navy-blue skirt that hugged her hips.

As she led him along a corridor to Magnus's office he couldn't help noticing also that she *had* lost some weight, but there was still a very womanly body under that figure-revealing skirt.

He'd always known she was a superficially attractive woman. Hell, he might as well admit it—physically he had always reacted to her. A male biological reflex that no doubt he shared with at least half of his gender group. Even Magnus hadn't been immune. And Magnus, in his peculiar innocence, had married her, probably not knowing how else to handle it when for the first time in his life, Steve suspected, he fell in love. With a woman half his age.

She went behind the desk that was unnaturally clear and tidy and sat down.

The high-backed leather chair looked too big for her. Steve supposed she was making a point. Magnus's office, Magnus's chair. The message was plain: I'm in charge now. She'd taken over.

Yet as he seated himself he had the feeling she was using the wide, solid desk as a shield. He supposed she might find his height and his rugby-broadened shoulders intimidating. He'd given up the game when he left New Zealand for America, but kept himself physically fit with running and weights, still influenced by Magnus's creed that a sluggish body led to a sluggish mind.

The boys were encouraged to develop their bodies as well as their minds, and Magnus expected them to put maximum effort into everything they did. He'd had no patience with laziness or incompetence.

It had been a tough regime but challenging, and those who survived were grateful. Witness the genuine sorrow at the funeral, grown men who had passed through Kurakaha as students breaking down in tears.

But not the widow.

She didn't look as though she'd shed a single tear since her husband's death, the blue, blue eyes as clear and chilly as mountain water.

"There doesn't seem to be any way out of this," Triss said with no preamble. "I've obtained a second opinion from a different legal firm."

The day after her husband's funeral? She hadn't lost any time.

Briskly she continued, "Unless Magnus did make a later will after you left—and Nigel seems sure he didn't—we're stuck with this one. I appreciate your… willingness to do your part, and I'll keep in touch. Do you have an e-mail address where I can contact you? It would be more convenient than phoning when it may be the middle of the night where you are."

"Back up, there. It seems to me, reading that will, that Magnus expected me to live here."

She looked as if she'd smelled something bad. "You know he drew it up when you *were* living here. I'm sure he wouldn't expect you drop a lucrative career in America to fulfill an outdated whim."

"Magnus didn't operate on whims." Except once, maybe. When he'd brought home his much younger bride. "He was a stubborn old—" Steve checked himself. "He was stubborn and quixotic and he never liked to admit he was wrong—"

"Where do you get off criticizing him?" Triss flared. "After—"

"After all he did for me?" Steve said impatiently. "I have the greatest respect for Magnus and you know it, but that doesn't mean I never saw any fault in him."

Magnus had been temperamental and sometimes wrongheaded. He held a grudge with the fervor of a starving man clutching his last crust. And yet he could be extraordinarily generous. And he had devoted considerable resources of time, money and energy to nurturing natural brilliance found in the most unlikely places.

"So what's your point?"

Okay, let her have it straight. "Magnus had his reasons and I have to respect them. I'm coming back here to live," he told her.

From the way she stared, her deceptively lovely mouth parted in shock, he knew she couldn't think of anything to say.

"It's what Magnus wanted," he said. "I'll fly back to L.A. in the next day or two to pack and organize things over there, then I'll be moving in."

"You can't do that!" She'd found her voice, and it sounded almost panic stricken.

"Why not?" His eyes narrowed. "What have you got to hide?"

"Nothing! But…there's no place for you here!"

Deliberately he stared her down, not caring now if he was intimidating, even hoping that he might be. Although, he conceded reluctantly, she didn't scare easily. Letting the silence speak, he looked past her, out the window, and then back at her defiant eyes, which held a hint of cornered rabbit in their astonished depths.

"Then you'd better make one," he said. They both knew this place was way big enough to accommodate an extra person, the rooms reserved for tutors seldom fully occupied. There was always a spare space somewhere.

He pushed back his chair, ensuring this time he was the one to terminate the discussion. "I'll let you know when I've settled things over in L.A. Meantime—" he leaned forward so that he was towering over her in her chair "—you won't, of course, think of making any major decisions without me, will you?"

Straightening without hurry, he took a card from his breast pocket and flipped it onto the desk in front of her. ''My e-mail address and phone number are on there.''

It was very satisfying turning his back on her and strolling to the door. He didn't look at her again before closing it behind him.

Chapter Two

Triss found that her fingers had curled about a heavy diamond-cut glass paperweight on the desk.

It would have felt good to throw it at Steve's dark, arrogant head, but that would have given him the pleasure of knowing he could make her lose control, and anyway it was too late. She'd only damage the door and chip the paperweight.

Releasing it, she flexed her fingers, seeing with mild surprise the red marks on her palm left by the sharp angles of the glass.

She had cleared the desk just the day before, leaving only the paperweight, a desk set and a handsome leather blotter holder, all gifts from past students to Magnus.

It was a task she'd have had to tackle some time, and there'd been no point in putting it off.

Besides, she'd had a half-formed hope that among the long-term clutter that had piled even higher in the last weeks of her husband's illness might be something that would negate the unchanged will.

Before Steve arrived she hadn't given particular thought to which room to use for their meeting, but perhaps by leading him in here she had subconsciously been hoping for some sense of Magnus's presence to give her a much needed feeling of confidence.

Steve—real name Gunther Stevens, according to the formal language in Magnus's will—had been her enemy from the moment they met. She had tried to get on with him for Magnus's sake, but Steve had been determined not to help her bridge the gap. In the end the gulf had been so wide and so deep it was clear one of them would have to go. Even Magnus had to see that.

So why had he not seen that the will he had drawn up soon after his marriage could only lead to disaster?

"Magnus, Magnus…" Triss dropped her forehead into a supporting hand, leaning on the desk that had once been his. "My dear man, what were you thinking of?"

She was assailed by blinding panic—a sensation hauntingly familiar from the days after she had lost both her parents with brutal suddenness halfway through her teens. Magnus's death had not been unexpected, but the sense of abandonment and fear, of being adrift in a hostile, or at best indifferent world, was almost as strong.

Salt stung her eyes, but at a tentative knock on the door she straightened, fiercely blinking the tears away. She had held up thus far, and too many people depended on her for her to give way now. She would have liked to crawl into some quiet corner and cry for hours. Instead, her voice strong and steady, she called, "Come in."

A husky youth sauntered into the room, hands thrust into the pockets of baggy pants worn with a camouflage jacket.

"Yes, Piripi?"

"Me and the guys're just wondrin' if it's okay to have a game."

"A game?"

"Touch football."

"You're asking for permission?" Triss said, puzzled. "You know in free time you can play whatever you like."

Piripi looked down at his shabby, thick-soled trainers. "Well, y'know, with Magnus, ah—" he swallowed "—you might think…" He looked up manfully. "It's not like we don't care, Triss…"

"I know you care," Triss said gently. "Of course you do."

Under their tough exteriors the boys had almost worshipped the man who had rescued them from various kinds of privation. And they treated Triss with a touching mixture of respect for her as Magnus's wife and a sometimes bantering, sometimes confiding familiarity that they might have accorded to an older sister.

"Sitting around moping can't help Magnus," she told Piripi, "and he'd expect you all to get on with working hard and playing hard."

That had been his philosophy for the school, although for himself the playing part had never come easily. "It's been too quiet around here the last couple of days."

Relieved, Piripi grinned, then wiped the grin away,

evidently thinking it was unsuitable. He backed to the doorway and hesitated there. "You okay, Triss?"

His large brown eyes were concerned, so different from the barely concealed hostility in Steve's inflexible gray stare. She only hoped he hadn't known what an effort it had taken to give him back an unblinking stare of her own, concealing all sign of emotion—or weakness.

Tears threatened again at the boy's delicacy and regard for her feelings, but she made herself smile reassuringly. "I'll be fine, Piripi. Thank you for asking."

The smile faded as he closed the door, but a small warming glow remained, easing a little the bleak sorrow that enveloped her. Not having any brothers or sisters of her own, at Kurakaha she'd found the closest thing to a family that she'd known since she was Piripi's age, when her parents had been cruelly snatched from her. As she had been then, he and the others were bereft and bewildered, and probably scared. So was Triss, but she couldn't let anyone know it.

Minutes later a whoop and a yell told her the boys were enjoying their game. It would do them good. They'd been unnaturally sober since she'd broken the news to them, and in the midst of her own sorrow her heart went out to them. Poised on the brink of manhood, in many ways they were still children.

Losing Magnus would leave a huge gap in their lives, but it was up to her to help them carry on as Magnus would have wished. Maybe his death would even strengthen their desire to live up to the standards he'd set.

As it should hers. Triss squared her shoulders and forced herself out of the chair. She didn't have time for self-pity. There was still a lot to be done.

* * *

Three weeks later she received a short e-mail from Steve giving her a date for his return. Apparently a little over a month was enough time for him to sort out his affairs in America. Later he sent another note with his flight arrival time, adding that he should reach Kurakaha within an hour or two of touchdown.

Triss replied with an equally curt message saying she'd send Zed with the Kurakaha van to fetch him from the airport.

She had to hand it to him, he'd wasted no time taking up his new responsibilities. But her heart sank at the prospect of working with Steve, of having him in the same house. Huge though it was, they would inevitably see each other every day.

Maybe he'd get bored quickly and return to the high life he must have become accustomed to. With any luck he would soon see that he could leave the place in her care with a clear conscience. She had every intention of demonstrating just how much she and Kurakaha didn't need him.

So it was a pity that he arrived in the middle of a crisis.

The boys had been released from their classes for the day and Triss was in what she still thought of as Magnus's office, writing by hand necessary letters to people who had sent condolences and ignoring with a practiced ear the sounds of a rowdy game of some kind outside.

When the quality of the shouts and catcalls changed, it took a few seconds to register, but as soon as she recognized the difference she shoved her chair back and left the room at a run.

By the time she reached the grassy playing field at the rear of the house a tutor was sprinting toward the

bunch of boys in the center of the field who appeared
to be randomly attacking each other with fists and feet.
The tutor tried to pull one from the mob and was felled
by a punch to his nose. Bleeding, he crawled away
from the kicking feet that threatened to trample him
and sat up, fishing for a handkerchief.

Infusing her voice with as much authority as she
could muster, Triss yelled at the combatants, *"Stop
it!"*

They didn't. The brawny seventeen-year-old Piripi
had one of his slighter fellows in a headlock, and the
victim's face was going blue.

Triss grabbed at Piripi's arm and shouted his name.

His grip eased when he recognized her, allowing the
other boy to slip from his grasp. The boy rounded,
wildly swinging a fist that missed its target, and Triss
felt his knuckles connect with her cheekbone, sending
her sprawling.

The sky seemed to revolve above her, her face had
gone numb and for a moment she wasn't sure what
had happened.

Groggily she got to her knees. The tutor was on his
feet, holding a bloodied handkerchief to his nose, and
now offered her his other hand. "Are you all right?"

Triss shook him off impatiently. "The fire hose,"
she gasped. "Piripi's going to kill that kid!"

Piripi, in the midst of the melee, had his opponent
on the ground and seemed intent on beating him to a
pulp.

While the tutor ran for the hose, Triss threw herself
at Piripi's back, getting her arms around his throat from
behind and screaming in his ear. "That's enough! Stop
it *now!*"

She felt the bunching of his shoulder muscles

against her breasts, and wondered if he'd turn on her, but instead he went suddenly slack, breathing hard. Then she heard over all the grunts and yells a deep, definitely adult masculine voice demanding, ''What the hell are you doing?'' And strong hands grasped and pulled her away just before a hard, cold, drenching spray descended, instantly soaking her blue faux-silk blouse and linen skirt.

Piripi shot upright, squinting and raising an arm against the force of the water.

The hand about Triss's arm jerked her aside and dragged her several yards from the still-struggling mob, leaving her there.

Wiping her eyes clear, through the spray she saw Steve haul up two wrestling boys from the ground and drive them apart, while Zed dealt with a couple of others, roaring at them to get their effing a's out of there before he gave those same a's the kicking their owners deserved.

Under the combined effect of two big, commanding men and the fire hose wielded by the tutor, the mini-riot was quickly quelled. The tutor turned off the hose, and Zed, his brown eyes shooting fire, ordered the culprits off to their rooms to change into dry clothes and warned them they needn't think this was the end of it.

Dragging wet hair off her face, Triss stood trying not to shiver, and when Steve approached her, his casual shirt and slacks also soaked, his hair darker than ever and sleeked to his head, she folded her arms about herself so that he wouldn't notice how unsteady she felt.

The movement drew his eyes, and the flicker of his long lashes made her look down, flushing as she saw how the water had plastered the thin fabric to her breasts, outlining not only her low-cut lace bra but what was only too clearly underneath it.

"Sorry you walked into that," she said, bringing his gaze back to her face.

"God knows what would have happened if we hadn't," Steve said. "What the hell did you think you were doing," he reiterated, "jumping into the thick of it?"

"Preventing a possible murder," Triss retorted. "Or manslaughter at the least. We were getting the situation under control."

"It didn't look under control to me."

"I'm sure we'd have managed, but thanks for your help."

"Managed how? By getting yourself beaten up?"

"They wouldn't hurt me."

One dark brow lifted slightly. "Then what's this?" His voice had roughened, and he raised a hand, the pad of his thumb barely brushing her cheek just below her left eye before he dropped his hand and his eyes narrowed to metallic slits. "Who hit you?"

Maybe the injury was worse than she'd realized, because despite the lightness of his fleeting touch she felt her skin tingle. "An accident. It doesn't matter."

"It matters."

"Thank you for your concern. Although I can't imagine why you're bothered." It wasn't as though he'd ever cared about her.

"I guess," he drawled, "I picked up Magnus's passion for perfection. I don't like to see a beautiful thing damaged."

The first time she'd ever heard anything like a compliment from him, although it hadn't sounded like one. "Thank you," she said, lacing her tone with irony to match his. "But I might remind you that I'm not a thing."

Maybe the inclination of his head was an acknowledgment, certainly not an apology. His gaze returned to her sodden blouse. "You'd better change," he said abruptly, "or when the boys see you again you might have another riot on your hands. Is that what started them off?"

Taken aback, Triss said, "I got wet when we turned the hose on them to stop the fight!"

"You don't need to be wet to set adolescent hormones in motion. But then," Steve added with a deadly mockery in his tone, "you'd know that, wouldn't you?"

Not sure what he was getting at, except that he was baiting her, Triss opened her mouth to ask him just what he meant, but before she got the chance Zed joined them, wringing out the wet shirt he'd taken off. "What was that all about?" he asked Triss.

"I've no idea. I was in the office when I heard it start. Is Arthur all right?" She'd seen Zed take the tutor's arm as he shuffled back to the house.

"He'll live. Nothing broken."

"Has this happened before?" Steve asked.

Zed shrugged. "There's been the odd fight, you know how they are. They don't usually all get into it at once."

Triss said, "They've been through a trauma, and all of them have been trying to be on their best behavior for too long. They're emotionally off balance."

Steve looked at her sharply. "You can't let them get away with it."

Wearily she wiped a trickle of water from her forehead before it reached her eyes. The last couple of months had been no picnic for her either. "I'll talk to them after dinner."

"I'll do it."

Her head lifted. "No." Did he think he could just walk in and take over? "They don't know you."

"They're going to. I might as well introduce myself, and make it clear that from now on we don't tolerate any violence."

"We never have! I'm sure this won't happen again."

"I wouldn't count on it. Young men are pack animals. They've lost their alpha male, and they need to know there's someone around to take his place. Until they accept there's a new chief there's going to be a lot of testing going on."

"And you're telling me you're going to be the new chief?" She didn't even attempt to hide the sarcasm in her voice.

Steve leveled an iron-gray gaze at her. "I don't say it's a good thing, but it's the way young males operate, especially in groups. Remember, I used to be one."

"They've been perfectly fine with me!" In fact most of them had been rather sweetly protective. Although a couple of tutors had complained about a lack of attentiveness and decreased motivation, with the occasional outburst of defiance and foul language.

"You're a woman," Steve said, as though that explained everything.

"So?"

"The first phase is over. They won't challenge you directly, but they're getting restive, and the next step will be to see how far they can go."

"Then I'll deal with it."

"*We* will deal with it," Steve said. "We're in this together, Triss." In his tone she heard the rider, *And I don't like it any more than you do.* "If they're not given the message about who's in charge here now, one of them will emerge as kingpin and we'll have a hell of a job on our hands. They're barely out of childhood and some of them are only half civilized."

"You've been reading *Lord of the Flies,*" she accused, surprising a half smile out him.

"Not lately," he said. "But we don't want someone's head stuck on a stake around here, and I'd certainly prefer it not to be mine—or yours. We have to make this work, Triss."

He was right about that, she supposed. Zed gave an approving nod, and Triss sighed. The men were closing ranks. Magnus himself had believed that boys needed strong male role models. Perhaps that was why he had inexplicably failed to alter his will, despite the long estrangement between him and his protégé. "Do you think it's a good idea," she queried Steve, "to start your…tenure by giving them a telling off?"

"If I stand by while you do it, they'll think I'm a wuss. Then we'll both be in deep trouble."

Unwillingly she capitulated with a small shrug, knowing that however unpalatable she found it, he was probably right. "I'm not the only one who needs a change of clothes," she observed. Casting a glance over his own wet shirt and trousers, she couldn't help noticing he looked as fit and leanly muscular as ever despite his presumably easy lifestyle. "We've put you in the annex.'' It was a self-contained one-bedroom unit adjoining the main house. "I'll take you—"

"I know where it is."

Of course he did. "We'll see you at dinner, then,'' she said. "Six-thirty in the dining room."

Triss and Magnus had always eaten together with the students and any tutors who chose to live in. Most of the current tutors preferred to commute from the city, and Arthur had taken his swollen nose home for his wife's ministrations. Zed would be giving his children their evening meal in their own cottage while his wife fixed dinner at the house, helped by two of the boys rostered for kitchen duty.

One of the helpers looked the worse for wear, and all the boys were subdued. Triss saw that an extra hand in the kitchen was needed, and was ladling soup into bowls at the pass-through counter when Steve entered and took his place in the small queue.

"Thanks,'' he said when she handed him a steaming bowl. "Anywhere?"

"Anywhere,'' she confirmed. The tables were round, and as Magnus had made a point of sitting at a different place each evening, Triss had been relieved of any awkwardness over a special chair after his death.

She still missed his presence though, and was sure the boys did, too.

Steve chose a table and she assumed he was introducing himself, but before she sat down with her own bowl of soup at another table she rapped a spoon on the glass and waited for the subdued hum of talk to stop.

Some of the faces turned toward her were apprehensive, a few belligerent, and several showed swellings and bruises. She'd held an ice pack to her own cheekbone until it stung and then numbed, and used a cover-up makeup, but the spot was tender and slightly swollen.

"Some of you will have met Mr. Stevens," she said, nodding toward Steve. At least a few had "met" him under less than friendly circumstances. "He's a trustee of the House now, and he'll be living here and helping out for a while." She didn't look to see what Steve made of that last bit. "I'm sure you'll all make him welcome. After dinner he'd like to speak to you in the common room. So be there. Thanks." They knew it was an order, not a matter of choice.

Triss didn't have much appetite. The day had been stressful, and she discovered that her cheek throbbed when she chewed. She left the crusty bread on her plate and, after the soup, settled for potatoes, mashed carrots and gravy.

Whatever the boys were expecting, it didn't seem to affect their need for food. Afterward they trooped into the room next door, where they lounged on chairs and a sofa or sprawled on the floor, with or without the cushions and bean bags provided.

Steve took a stance where they could all see him and simply waited in silence for them to stop shoving and joshing each other and fall quiet.

"When I arrived this afternoon," he began, "I thought I'd entered a war zone."

Uncertain laughter came from some of the boys. But Steve's face was stern, his voice uncompromising. "Magnus would never have stood for that kind of thing and you all know it. If it happens again, anyone who takes part will be asked to leave. Is that clear?"

Shuffles and muttered acknowledgments.

"At least one of you owes Triss an apology," Steve added grimly. "In fact it might not be a bad idea if you all apologized to her for your behavior this afternoon before you leave. But don't go yet."

He paused. One boy, arms folded, was tipping his chair dangerously far back, apparently ignoring Steve. After a few seconds the boy looked up, locked gazes with the man for a long moment, then let the chair thud into place.

Steve's glance swept the room. "Magnus made both me and his wife trustees under his will," he said. "That's why I'm here, to carry out his work. You guys are lucky—you won't know how lucky until after you leave. A lot of you haven't had it easy up until now. We don't promise you ever will, but we'll do our damnedest to make sure you have the skills to make the most of what you have."

Magnus's creed, Triss thought, watching Steve catch each boy's eyes in turn.

"I'm an old boy of Kurakaha myself, so don't think I can't understand your problems—and don't think you can get away with anything either. I know all the tricks because I've pulled most of them myself."

That drew another reluctant laugh and some assessing looks.

"I'm not going to bore you with long speeches.

Anyone wants to talk to me, I'll be around. I'm going to be around for a long time.''

Triss guessed that last was aimed at her.

Steve had impressed the boys, not so much by what he said as the way he said it, with unmistakable authority, his manner firm but approachable. Even the easy way he stood as he talked to them, neither parade-ground straight nor slouching, proclaimed confidence in his control of any situation. They'd reserve judgment but he'd made a good start.

The students began filing out, each one stopping to mutter an apology to her. ''You'd better apologize to Mr. Gill,'' she told the one who had punched the tutor. ''If he comes back after what happened to him this afternoon.''

''Yeah, awright. Didden know it was him.'' The boy slouched off.

When they had all left, Steve looked across the room at Triss. ''How did I do?''

Surprised that he'd asked, and trying hard not to sound grudging, she said, ''Very well. You don't think we might have asked what started them off?''

''A disputed goal, the guys at my table told me. Any excuse to let off steam.'' He grinned faintly. ''Tears are shameful, but a good brawl can have a cathartic effect.''

Triss wondered if the forceful way he'd helped Zed break up the fight had been cathartic for him, too. She recalled the way he'd looked when he approached her afterward, his hair sleeked to his scalp and the wet shirt molding powerful shoulders and a broad chest. His face had been taut and energized, his eyes glinting like new metal, even before they'd taken in the revealing nature of her own wet clothes. When the glint had altered to a very specific and personal appraisal.

She swallowed, shaking off a ripple of disturbing sensation.

"Thanks for the intro at dinner," Steve was saying.

"We always introduce guests...or new staff." She paused. "You might have consulted me before threatening to throw them out."

"Only if the same thing happened again. However," he added, "point taken."

And no sense in laboring it. Politely she asked, "I hope the annex is okay? If there's anything you need let me know."

"It's fine. When can we go over the books?"

"The books?"

"Annual reports and balance sheets. I'd like to know what's been happening over the past few years, and what exactly our financial situation is."

"I can tell you that." He knew she had been keeping the accounts ever since arriving at Kurakaha. She was just about to graciously concede that of course he could see the records if he wished, when he added, his voice unmistakably hardening, "I'd like to see them, all the same. And I'll be bringing in an independent auditor."

Triss went cold, then hot. The skin over her cheekbones burned, the bruised one throbbing painfully in time with the thudding of her heart that seemed to be hurting, too. "You don't trust me."

"I didn't say that." But he wasn't saying he did, either.

"The books are audited every year."

"I'm sure. Who chose the auditor?"

She wouldn't dignify that with an answer. "You're welcome to go through them," she said stiffly. "You and your auditor."

She felt like flying at him, starting a small private brawl of her own. Instead she wheeled and left him, not trusting herself to stay any longer in the same room.

After checking that the boys on kitchen duty were clearing up and laying the tables for breakfast, she made sure the cook didn't need any other help, and marched out into the gardens. Already a couple of pale stars hung in the sky, and a gleaming sickle moon had risen over the trees.

Moving away from the house and avoiding Zed's cottage, she took a path under the trees. It was darker here but she knew every inch of the grounds, and her stride didn't slacken as she followed a winding course up a slope, until the path ended at a tiny stone building covered in climbing vines and holding a wooden seat just big enough for two.

Once, she supposed, it had been a spot for lovers, before Magnus bought the house and grounds from the descendants of the man who had built it at the beginning of the twentieth century.

She came here when she needed a break from the constant demands on her time and energy. The boys were interesting, always stimulating, sometimes riotous, sometimes poignant and often exhausting. A few moments to herself were rare and precious. Sometimes lately she'd felt it was all too much—the house too big, its inhabitants too volatile, and everyone expecting too much of her.

In daylight the arched doorway of the grotto allowed a glimpse through trees of the farmlands beyond, and cars streaming to and from Auckland along the motorway in the distance. There were moments when she longed to join them, escape from the tyranny of responsibility that had fallen on her shoulders. Steve was here now to share it, but his hostile presence only imposed more stress.

It was getting dark, the cars intermittent flashes of light, far away, and she closed her eyes, leaning her head against the cool stone and trying to think of nothing.

Which was difficult, because Steve's strong, handsome features and condemning, metallic scrutiny kept getting in the way.

After a while she opened her eyes, and immediately sat up straight with a gasp that was almost a scream.

A tall, broad-shouldered figure loomed in the narrow arched doorway, blocking what remained of the fading light.

Chapter Three

"Were you asleep?" Steve said.

Recognizing his voice should have reassured her, but instead Triss's heart was hammering, her body rigid with tension. He added, "I thought you'd have seen me coming up the path."

"I wasn't asleep, but I didn't see you. What are you doing here?"

There was a pause before he answered. "Renewing my acquaintance with the place. What about you?" He raised an arm, his hand resting on the stone arch.

"I come here quite often. To think."

"Sorry I disturbed you." But he didn't move. Nor did he sound particularly sorry.

There was no reason to feel threatened. Only, the grotto was very small, and although he hadn't actually entered, he was big and in her way if she wanted to leave.

Of course he'd step aside if she made a move to go.

But somehow she was reluctant to put that to the test. And while she debated Steve spoke again.

"Why didn't you tell me Magnus was ill?" he asked harshly.

"He didn't want anyone to know."

The dark bulk of his shoulders shifted impatiently. "You knew."

"I'm...I was his wife." Of course she'd known. It was she who had persuaded him to see a doctor.

"Was it his heart?"

"Yes, in the end. He'd been...failing, and he was in hospital after having what they called 'an episode' but we thought he was recovering. Then...it was quite sudden."

Steve half turned, but only to lean his shoulders against the frame of the arch, arms folded. "So you must have had time to make plans, if he'd been sick for a while."

"Plans?"

"You don't really want to stay here, surely? Even though you get more in cash if you do. He left you the bulk of his money. I'd advise you to take it and run."

Triss shot to her feet. "I didn't ask for any advice from you, and I certainly don't need it!" And the raw feeling in her throat was caused by anger, not hurt at his callous, unjust assumptions. "Excuse me, I'd like to go back to the house."

For a long second or two she thought he wasn't going to move. Refusing to wait on his pleasure, and in a dire need to get away, she made to push through the narrow space he'd left her, miscalculated and felt her breasts brush against his shirt as she tried to pass him.

Steve straightened a little too late. Triss stumbled

over his foot, and his hands closed about her upper arms.

For a moment they stood together in the stone doorway, bodies touching, Steve's chin only an inch from her temple. She could hear—even feel—the harsh intake of his breath, smell clean clothing and soap and a faint, frighteningly seductive male skin-scent.

In irrational panic she clenched her fists and raised them, thumping his chest. "Let me go!"

He swung her to the outside of the doorway with easy strength, then released her, saying, "Glad to, but are you're sure that's what you want?"

The implied suggestion was outrageous. Fury banished fear and she raised a fist again, aiming at his face.

He grabbed her wrist before it connected, holding her away from him. "I wouldn't try it. You won't win."

Triss tugged against his grip and he retained it just long enough to make her aware that he was right, even if she employed some of the self-defense techniques that had momentarily flown right out of her mind. He was bigger and much stronger, and they both knew he was on his guard and would easily defeat her in a physical tussle.

When he removed his hand she stepped back, resisting the temptation to rub at her numbed wrist. Thank heaven there were no witnesses to this little contretemps.

Chagrined, she said, stiff-lipped, "I shouldn't have tried to hit you." Normally a totally nonviolent person, she had been goaded to the point of unthinkingly hitting out.

"Damn right you shouldn't," Steve agreed. "Never underestimate your opponent. Fortunately I'm not in the habit of fighting with women."

Not physically. But he had no compunction about attacking them with words. It hadn't escaped her that he was not apologizing for that. "Do they often hit you?" she inquired.

The quick flash of his white teeth in the darkness resembled a snarl more than a smile. "You're the first and only."

"You surprise me," Triss said. Then she turned her back and walked away from him.

Steve watched her retreat into the darkness. She'd left him to it, king of the hill, and he should be savoring the victory. Instead he felt bleak and empty and annoyingly in the wrong.

He hadn't assaulted her, he reminded himself, hadn't even retaliated when she went for him with her fist.

She could have waited for him to give way when she said she wanted to leave, but no—she'd deliberately brushed against him in the narrow opening, setting his pulses on fire with a familiar, unwilling desire, and when he'd saved her from falling on her face, she'd made a show of fighting him off as if he'd made an unwelcome advance.

Then, flying into a rage when he made it clear he wasn't interested, she'd tried to sock him on the jaw.

She would find that he wasn't as easily manipulated as the half-grown males she'd been around in the past few years.

In his own formative years he'd not had much to do with women, but he was more experienced now. Triss

herself had taught him a thing or two, and after moving
to L.A. and becoming involved in the fringes of the
entertainment business, he'd seen the way some
women used their looks and their wits to advantage,
twisting strong, powerful men around apparently fragile, pretty little fingers.

It had worked with Magnus, but Steve was determined that no woman—and especially this woman—
was going to have him dancing to her dangerous tune.
He might not have been a match for her years ago, but
she'd find it harder to get rid of him this time round.

After breakfast Triss invited Steve, in as cordial a
voice as she could muster, to come to her office any-
time and she'd have the yearly accounts ready for him.

"*Your* office? Or Magnus's?"

"My office," she replied firmly, knowing he was
wondering if already she'd appropriated for herself the
room that had always been her husband's domain.
"Down the corridor and just about opposite his."
When Steve had left she'd still been doing the accounts
on a table in Magnus's upstairs flat, but for years now
she'd had her own office.

He nodded and she left him finishing his second cup
of coffee.

When he arrived she had a pile of folders on the
desk. Laying the last one on top as he entered, she told
him, "These are printouts from previous years. This
year's accounts are on disk and in my computer." The
machine sat on her desk, a much newer piece of fur-
niture than Magnus's kauri antique.

Steve looked around at the filing cabinets, the
shelves neatly stacked with file boxes, and the typing

chair behind the desk, as if noting the contrast between this businesslike room and the chaos Magnus had worked in. He picked up the folders. "Do you mind if I use Magnus's desk?"

It was a reasonable request. There wasn't much room in the annex to sort through papers, and the bigger office would be private and convenient. Triss had the feeling he was staking a claim, but without an excuse she'd look churlish and petty if she refused. At least he'd had the decency to ask.

"If you like," she said, as graciously as she could. "I may need to fetch some documents from time to time but I'll try not to disturb you."

He nodded and seemed about to leave. She realized he was looking at the darkened bruise below her eye, that makeup had failed to disguise. Abruptly he asked, "Is that painful?"

"Less so than yesterday. It'll fade."

After he'd gone away with the files, she let her head fall into her hands and raked her fingers through her hair, wishing passionately that the world would just go away for at least a day or two. And take Steve with it.

But there were bills to be paid and people to be contacted. The annual budget to be prepared. Tutors to be found for next year's program, a task that had to be done way ahead of time. It was going to become a major problem without Magnus's personal connection with an extensive network of people ranging from musicians and special educators to politicians, philanthropists and the heads of various educational and musical institutions and youth aid programs.

Sighing, Triss switched on the computer. But her

mind was still with the man in the room across the way.

Steve had come far since Magnus had plucked him up from the street when he was a teenager, playing experimental music on a cheap secondhand keyboard that he'd repaired himself.

Under Magnus's wing he'd learned a lot about the technique and theory of music while pursuing his interest in electronically produced sound. Before he was out of his teens he had been building his own digital instruments, at first from cheap used parts, and selling them. By the time Triss arrived at Kurakaha he'd been tutoring part-time, maintaining the House's electronic equipment and using an outbuilding for his own lucrative small business.

Magnus had tolerated that as the price of having Steve within his little kingdom, but had never given up trying to persuade him to make music rather than its instruments.

Then a visiting American businessman had been impressed enough to lure Steve to Los Angeles with the offer of a partnership that Steve accepted against Magnus's determined opposition, and there had been raised voices before Steve packed and left. Within two years he had bought his partner out. Since then the firm had earned a reputation for cutting-edge technology and made him a rich man.

Steve didn't spend all his time examining the books. Triss discovered that he'd looked in on several classes, and a few times over the next couple of weeks she saw him chatting with some of the boys, playing cards in the rec room or giving a few brawny lads an informal rugby coaching session.

He helped Zed lop dead branches from trees and saw them into firewood, and spent an entire day pruning bushes that had got out of hand. Another day the two men walked all around the building, pointing and discussing for hours.

And sometimes he shut himself into one of the music rooms, apparently working on some project with one of the electronic synthesizers he'd donated to the House some years before.

He didn't discuss anything with Triss until the day he came into her office holding one of the folders she'd handed over to him and said, "I'd like to look at the latest figures. Can you print them out for me?"

"I'm a bit busy right now," she said truthfully. "Can it wait until tomorrow?"

"What are you doing?"

"You're not my employer, Steve."

"No, I'm your fellow trustee. Of course, if you're working on some private business of your own…"

"I don't have any!" Triss snapped. Kurakaha was the only business she had time for. "I'm sorting out a budget for next year."

"Shouldn't we be conferring on that?"

"This is a draft," she told him. "I'll let you have a copy as soon as I've finished." She hoped he wouldn't cavil just for the sake of being difficult. "Perhaps you should finish going over the financial reports before we discuss the budget."

"You're probably right," he conceded. "We certainly need to talk. I have a number of questions but I'll wait until I have all the figures."

"I'll be happy to clarify anything in there that you don't follow."

"Oh, I think I follow all right. It's not so much what's there as what isn't."

Triss's brow creased. "I don't know what you mean."

"I'm not in a position to comment yet," he said, "but I'll definitely be asking for an outside opinion."

"You won't find anything wrong!"

"Then you have nothing to worry about, do you?"

Long after he'd left her Triss was still shaking with anger. How dare Steve question her integrity? He'd never liked her, she knew that, but suspecting her of dishonesty—of cheating Magnus and the boys—was beyond dislike.

After finishing for the day she printed out the papers Steve wanted and knocked on the door of the annex. Getting no answer, she tried the door, found it unlocked and stepped inside.

There was no real kitchen, only a sink counter and a small fridge and microwave. Another counter separated them from a living area furnished with a couple of comfortable chairs and a sofa flanking a low table. A cheap kitchen table with two chairs tucked under it served as either a desk or for dining.

The bedroom with its own en suite bathroom opened off the living room. A come-down from what Steve was accustomed to, Triss supposed, walking across the room to deposit the papers on the table.

Half a dozen cardboard boxes were stacked in a corner behind the sofa. She wondered if he would get around to unpacking them before he tired of the place and went back to his glamorous life in America.

He'd already filled the built-in bookcase along one wall. Never able to resist books, she made a slight detour on her way out to take a closer look at one, then pulled the book from the shelf to read the back copy.

The door opened and she glanced up guiltily as Steve closed it behind him.

"I brought this year's monthly reports for you," she said quickly. "They're on the table."

He was still standing before the door. His eyes went from her to the bookcase, definitely not on the path to the exit. "And…?"

"Sorry." She indicated the book she'd been looking at. "One of my favorite authors. I couldn't help noticing her name." She hastily replaced it.

"Borrow it if you haven't read it," he invited, walking forward. He drew the book out again as she moved aside. "Here."

Triss hesitated and he said, "It's not booby-trapped."

She took the book. "Aren't you afraid I might steal it?"

His eyes were thoughtful, assessing. "I haven't accused you of anything."

"Yet."

His gaze narrowed. "Are you afraid I'll have cause to?"

"No!"

"Then let's say I'm reserving judgment."

"But you'd like to find evidence to hang me!"

"And ruin that lovely neck?" He let his eyes drift down momentarily, and she felt the pulse at the base of her throat kick into hurried life, as if he'd touched it. "You're being melodramatic, Triss."

She wished her name didn't sound so much like a caress on his lips. Even the sardonic note he injected into it didn't stop her feeling an odd shiver of... pleasure, she realized, instinctively recoiling.

"I'm not going to touch you." Steve wheeled from her, reinforcing the unspoken suggestion that he'd find that loathsome. "I need a beer. What can I get you?"

"Nothing, I was just leaving." It shouldn't matter that he didn't like her, but an old bewildered hurt made her voice husky, and pride demanded that she get out before he guessed at her feelings.

He was striding to the fridge under the counter, opening it. A beer can in his hand, he said, "Sit down. It's time we talked."

"It's time you developed some manners!" Although she had to admit that normally he was scrupulous about observing the conventions. At least if she fought with him she wasn't likely to burst into the tears that were too close to the surface these days, a humiliation she couldn't bear to have him witness.

He turned and straightened. "I just invited you to have a drink with me."

"You just *ordered* me to sit down."

Steve looked exasperated, then he gave her a curt nod. "Triss, please sit down. I have something to discuss, if you don't mind. It's important."

He appeared to be making an attempt not to sound too heavily sarcastic. And the blessed spurt of temper had dispelled her urge to cry. Perhaps if they talked they could come to some kind of agreement, even if only to keep out of each other's way.

She subsided into one of the armchairs. "I'll have juice if you've got any."

"Is apple okay?"

She said yes, and he poured it into a glass, sipping his beer from the can when he sat down opposite her.

"The bruise has gone," he remarked, inspecting her face. "You'll be relieved."

"It was nothing." She raised a hand to where it had been. "What did you want to talk about?"

He seemed to be still appraising her face, but after a moment he said, "The boys have noticed we're not getting along."

He lifted the beer can again to his lips and tipped it. She watched the movement of his throat above an open shirt collar, and pulled her gaze away. "We've never quarreled in front of them."

"They're not stupid. They know we're avoiding each other."

"Does it matter?" Triss asked. "As long as we don't let our…as long we don't let it interfere with the running of the House," she amended.

"It bothers them. Friction at the top makes them feel insecure." He sat back, cradling the can in one long-fingered hand. "We've seen the result of that before. And they're likely to try playing us off against each other."

"There was no friction before you came!"

Steve looked at her, his eyes almost colorless, all expression wiped out of them. "I could turn that back at you."

A long time ago Triss had been the newcomer, the interloper, and Steve hadn't liked it. Obviously he still resented her presence here. She was fairly sure that her advent had been a factor in his decision to leave. But that had turned out well for him.

She lifted her glass and sipped the cool drink.

"We need to spend more time together," Steve said. "Show a united front."

Triss shrugged. Reluctantly taking his point, she said, "I'll try if you will."

"Don't try too hard," he said dryly. "We're supposed to be friends, not lovers."

Chapter Four

Triss tensed. The word *lovers* had shocked her, even in the negative, raising a disturbing, half-formed picture in her mind.

"I'll do my best," she promised, dismissing the bizarre image of herself and Steve locked in each other's arms. "But it's difficult to be friends when you don't trust me."

"Do you trust *me?*" Steve demanded.

"I never thought you were dishonest." She gave him a challenging look.

"Don't you think you're jumping to conclusions?"

"*I* am?"

"I'm just trying to figure out where all the money's gone. Magnus's money."

"Magnus hadn't earned money for years, except from his investments. And the House is expensive to run."

"Zed says it should be reroofed soon, and there are

a number of repairs beyond his handyman skills that need to be attended to.''

"Expenses keep going up, income's gone down. You must have seen that in the accounts.''

He didn't reply, nursing his beer can and looking at her with coolly skeptical eyes.

Triss said, "Get your own accountant to check it out.''

"I will.''

He wasn't going to give an inch. She finished her drink and stood up. "Thanks." Her voice was clipped. "I'll be going.''

"What are you planning to do now?''

Triss looked at her watch. "I may take a walk before dinner." After working at the computer all day she needed to clear her head and release some of the tension from her body. There was a faint throbbing at her temples. "Why?''

"Maybe I should come with you.''

"What for?''

"A show of togetherness, remember? The boys will see us leave and come back together.''

"Oh, all right," Triss capitulated. If they were going to put on an act she supposed they might as well start now. "I need to change and put on some walking shoes." She was wearing a skirt and blouse, but for walking she'd prefer jeans.

"I'll meet you at the front door.''

Where they'd be most visible to anyone who happened to be about. Triss nodded and he opened the door to let her out.

Jeans were not an invitation to seduction, Steve reminded himself as Triss descended the steps ahead of him. But he couldn't help admiring the way her trim yet distinctly feminine behind moved inside them. Quickly he went down himself and strode to her side, shoving his hands firmly into his pockets to remove the temptation to touch.

Triss held her head up, eyes straight, going quickly along the broad drive and out the wide gateway. There wasn't a great deal of traffic because the road was a dead end, most of the properties along it being small farms.

Cattle cropping the lush grass in the paddocks paused to stare as Triss and Steve passed, a few ambling over to the fence to watch, while sheep lifted their aristocratic noses and skittishly ran away.

A gusty breeze blew Triss's hair about her face, and she shook the fine strands back, lifting a hand to tuck them behind her ear.

Steve glanced at her. "Your hair used to be much longer."

"I've grown older, and it's less trouble to care for this way."

She hadn't grown any less beautiful, Steve thought. It would have been easier if she had. He'd known many other beautiful women in the last several years, yet he still felt the reluctant tug of irresistible attraction every time he looked at her. An attraction tempered by anger that gnawed at him, a deep, hidden canker.

"It's time I had it cut again," Triss went on, and Steve just stopped himself from saying, No, don't do that!

He dug his hands into his pockets and increased the length of his stride, frowning at the hard surface of the road, edged with delicate white heads of Queen Anne's lace, tangled honeysuckle and tiny blue and pink wild-flowers peeking from swaying grasses.

It wasn't until they'd breasted a hill and were look-ing down on the red and green roofs of farm houses fenced from the surrounding grazing land, and a nar-row river winding between the willows and tree ferns along its banks, that he realized Triss was slightly breathless.

"You should have said I was going too fast," he told her, coming to an abrupt halt.

"I'm all right." She wasn't looking at him, her eyes fixed on the view before them.

Nearby a huddle of large gray rocks nestled among the roadside flowers. Steve took Triss's arm. "Here."

He thought she was going to resist, but then the tensed muscles beneath his fingers relaxed and she let him lead her to the rocks and push her gently down onto the flattest of them.

Steve sat on a lower one, leaning his back against the rock she sat on and stretching his long legs out. "I'd forgotten what this landscape was like," he said. The exotic trees had colored up for autumn, but the small darker islands of native bush would remain stub-bornly green all winter.

"What's it like where you live?" Triss asked.

"I live here now," he reminded her.

After a short silence she said, "I mean in America. Los Angeles. You wouldn't see many trees, would you?"

A safe subject, he supposed. "There are palm trees," he told her, "along the streets. Tall, skinny palm trees." He described the city and the surrounding hills with their brushy vegetation, and she seemed in-terested, perhaps in spite of herself. Answering her questions, he went on talking about places he'd seen, people he'd met.

"You'll miss it," she said.

"I'll miss some things, some people."

"Do you have a girlfriend there?"

Remembering this was Triss Allardyce, he looked up, wondering what agenda she was following now. She had her head turned away from him and seemed to be examining something on the surface of the rock beside her, a swathe of shining hair concealing her face.

"No," he said, and stood up. Automatically he extended a hand to her, but she ignored it, rising on her own and turning back the way they had come, walking quickly.

Steve fell into step beside her. "There's no rush," he said. "You wouldn't want to run yourself out of breath again."

"I don't want to be late for dinner. It would set a bad example."

He shot her a baffled glance. Did she really care about Kurakaha and its inhabitants? Certainly so far she'd given every appearance of doing so. The boys liked her, and she treated them with friendly affection, though occasionally curbing excess boisterousness with a firm no-nonsense approach.

f course she was older now than when she'd arrived at the House as Magnus's wife—into a milieu full of males nearer to her in age than her husband's. And perhaps some of his idealism had rubbed off on her after all. His charisma had influenced a lot of people.

Triss walked with her eyes on the road ahead, trying to ignore the man whose long legs easily kept pace. For some time neither of them spoke.

What had possessed her to ask that personal question of Steve? As soon as it left her lips she'd wanted to take it back. His curt answer and the closed look on his face as he'd stood up reinforced her discomfort.

It had occurred to her as they talked that maybe he'd left someone behind. Steve had always been good-looking, and with the years and his increasing success he'd grown in self-assurance, the added maturity making him even more attractive. He had money and a successful career on the fringe of the most glamorous occupation on earth. There must have been women in his life—surely it was surprising if he *wasn't* in a relationship.

"I didn't mean to intrude on your private life," she said, swallowing a lump of pride. "But when you mentioned there were people you'd miss, it seemed a logical question."

He shrugged. "As I said, the answer is no. I have no ties in America." She heard the unspoken corollary, *You're not getting rid of me easily.*

"Surely it will be difficult to run your business from here?"

"As you pointed out before, communication is pretty instant worldwide these days. And the business has grown to the stage where delegation is much easier. Though I still like to keep my hand in on the practical side. If I may have to spend time overseas occasionally, that's no big problem."

The expense of airfares across the world were apparently no object for him. "Lucky you," she murmured.

"I have been very lucky," he confirmed. "I owe Magnus my life."

"Your life?"

"You know what he did for me."

"I know you had no family and Magnus found you busking on a street corner."

"That's all?" When she nodded, Steve said, "He didn't say I'd been brought up in foster homes after my father went AWOL and my mother gave up living and took an overdose? Or that I'd been in trouble and was on probation at the time?"

"No."

"I called him a dirty old man when he first offered me a home, even threw it at him later when I knew it wasn't true. He never told you what an obnoxious brat I could be?"

Triss couldn't resist. "He didn't need to tell me."

Silence for a moment, then Steve gave a crack of laughter. "I guess I asked for that," he said. "But believe me, Magnus had a lot worse to put up with before he made a half-decent human being of me. I didn't trust anyone and I was sure he had some underlying motive, even if it was to make me into an upright citizen—not exactly a priority for me at the time."

"And yet he succeeded in doing it."

"As a side effect of developing what he saw as a potentially wasted gift. The only thing Magnus believed to be truly wicked was not using a talent to its utmost potential."

"I know. It was what made him unique. He never was your average do-gooder."

"It also meant people took advantage of him."

As he surely believed Triss had.

But was his own conscience clear? "He helped you, but you defied him in the end."

"There came a time when I had to choose my own path. It wasn't easy—I know he meant the best for me."

So at least he acknowledged that. "Was Magnus the only person you ever trusted?" she asked him. Because there certainly weren't many, and she was well aware she wasn't one of them.

Steve was quiet again for a second. She thought he wasn't going to answer until he finally said, "One of my foster mothers, but she got ill and they took me away. No one ever told me if she'd recovered or not. I guess the reason it didn't work out with my next foster family was I'd hated being taken away from her, so I was determined to be difficult. Yeah, I trusted her." He paused. "And a social worker who never lied to me. Because everyone else did."

"Everyone? That can't be true."

"Maybe not. But that's what I came to believe."

So he'd grown up with a chip on his shoulder. She should be sorry for him, but it wasn't easy to equate this assured and self-righteous man, who had shown her nothing but contempt and suspicion, with the mixed-up and no doubt emotionally damaged boy he had once been.

A car swept toward them. Triss returned the driver's wave and it slowed and stopped, the driver winding down the window to rest a muscular, tanned arm on the door frame. He was in his late thirties, with a mop of sandy curls and a friendly grin.

"Triss," he said. "How's things?"

"As well as we can expect, thanks Grant."

He nodded and removed his sympathetic gaze from her to look curiously at Steve.

Triss said, "This is Steve—I mean Gunther Stevens."

Steve cast her a quick look and went forward to shake the other man's outstretched hand. "Steve," he said firmly.

"Grant McKay," Triss completed the introduction. "He brings meat and fruit for us sometimes from his farm."

Grant squinted up at Steve. "You're the prodigal foster son," he said.

"Not officially. You must have moved into the valley after I left."

"Pretty soon after, I guess." Grant squinted up at him. "Shame about old Magnus. How long are you staying?"

"I'm not leaving," Steve replied. "I'm a trustee of the House."

"Yeah?" Grant's eyes went from him to Triss and back again, sizing Steve up. "Well…guess I'll be seeing you round, then. Uh…see ya, Triss."

She smiled at him and stepped back as the car moved off. When they resumed walking Steve gave her a piercing look, holding her eyes for a moment.

"What?" she said.

His brows lifted. "I didn't say anything."

But his eyes spoke a whole library. A law library, full of judgments in weighty tomes. Triss dragged her gaze away and began walking rapidly, her mouth tight. Dismayingly, she was close to tears again. Silently she cursed her wayward emotions, which had been much too close to the surface lately.

The wind was in her face now, and she kept her eyes open, letting it sting the tears away.

"I don't use my first name," he said.

She knew that. Until recently she hadn't even known what it was. "You don't care for 'Gunther'?"

"Not much. At school," he added with a faint grin, "the guys shortened it to Gun."

"It suits you."

He gave a low laugh. "Is that a crack?"

Triss bit her lip, slightly ashamed despite her spurt of defiance. "Just a comment," she said. "Your eyes…"

She was digging herself in deeper. Best stop now before she made complete hash of this.

"What about my eyes?"

"Nothing." Except that the way he focused on her sometimes, she could almost imagine crosshairs at the center of his vision. Intersecting right in the middle of her heart.

They were approaching the house, walking through the gateway. He said, "Your name's short for Theresa, isn't it? Wasn't she a saint?"

Triss glanced at him without speaking. She quickened her pace further.

His hand curling about her arm slowed her. "That wasn't a crack at you."

"What was it, then?" She wrenched her arm from his hold and turned to face him, lifting her chin to meet his eyes. There were no crosshairs there. Only a wary bafflement lurking in the depths.

"*Are* you a saint?" he asked.

What an extraordinary question, and he'd asked it almost as if he really wanted to know the answer. "Of course not!" Triss blinked at him. "I suppose that makes me a sinner."

"I don't know what it makes you," he said slowly.

Then, on a completely different note, ''Why did you marry Magnus?''

The question came like a bullet, straight down the barrel of his gunmetal stare.

It robbed her of breath, her heartbeat becoming painful and labored. The very fact that he'd asked shouted that the obvious, simple answer—that she'd loved her husband—had never occurred to him. And it was blindingly clear that if she gave it he wouldn't believe her.

Breathing carefully, Triss forced air into her lungs. Her eyes fixed and wide, she said, ''Why don't you work it out for yourself?''

He would anyway, to his own satisfaction, she told herself as she wheeled away from him and rapidly ascended the broad, shallow front steps. The big kauri door was open as usual, and she resisted a childish temptation to slam it in his face.

The passageway was dark but she didn't switch on any lights. Her hand was turning the doorknob of Magnus's study before she'd consciously decided where she was going.

She threw open the door, and in the fading light coming through the window she could see the folders she'd handed to Steve, scattered and piled on the desk. He'd taken over here.

Bitterness welled into her throat, mingled with an old, horribly familiar panic.

She'd never felt so alone in her life.

Retreating into the passageway, she closed the door and leaned her forehead momentarily on the cool panel of wood, reminding herself she was a grown woman, not a suddenly orphaned teenager anymore. Disinclined to move, she was deathly tired, but forced herself toward the dining room. *I don't want to be late for dinner,* she'd told Steve. He was probably there already, talking to the boys, laughing with them, inviting confidences.

It was easy for him. He didn't have to watch every word, weigh every smile, censor every sympathetic touch in case it might be misconstrued.

He was their new alpha male, who had once been where they were now, who'd made it.

Magnus had wanted that for the boys. Someone they could not only look up to but also identify with. A man.

Whatever his faults, there was no doubt Steve was all man. Anyone could see that. Pausing in the lighted doorway, she watched him as he listened to a couple of eager boys seated opposite him, a faint grin lifting the corners of his mouth. When the youngsters laughed he joined in.

A quick glance at the other side of the pass-through told her everything was under control, her help not needed. The boys lining up for their meals moved aside, letting her go first. It was a nice gesture that always warmed her. She took her plate of pie and vegetables and turned, deciding which table to sit at tonight. One was already full, but at another there was an empty chair next to Steve. As she hesitated he glanced up and his eyes homed on her face.

He made no move, but after a moment she found herself walking in that direction. He watched her, and she realized the boys had turned to follow his gaze. If she veered away now the snub would be obvious.

She kept walking and paused at the chair, the warm plate in her hands. Steve stood up and silently pulled out the chair, his eyes at close quarters quite dark and very enigmatic.

Triss sat down with a peculiar feeling of fatefulness. The trivial incident seemed to have acquired some kind of importance, as if her world had shifted slightly. Or at least the small, closed world of Kurakaha.

Which was all that mattered, really. She was simply keeping up appearances, as she and Steve had agreed to do.

He reached partway across her to hand a bottle of sauce to one of the boys, and his arm brushed against hers. The fork she'd picked up clattered onto her plate, but no one appeared to notice. Her eyes glazed as she took hold of it again. Steve gave a short, deep laugh of amusement, and she lifted her head sharply to look at him. But he was laughing at something one of the others had said, his hard profile turned away from her.

Just because she seemed to have an acute sensitivity to his lightest, most accidental touch, that didn't mean he shared it.

It was a female thing, she decided, cutting into the delicately browned pie crust. Throughout history women had needed to know who their enemies were, especially their bigger, stronger male enemies, so that they could take evasive action. They'd developed a sixth sense that told them which men were dangerous—it was that sixth sense that made her skin tingle whenever Steve came near, that quickened her pulses and shortened her breath. It was responsible for her awareness of his every gesture even when she wasn't looking at him, because over time women had survived by knowing when a man's sudden movement threatened their safety. It was bred in the genes of those who had lived long enough to pass it on to their girl children.

There were still women who lived like that every minute of the day.

Triss shivered, and swallowed a piece of pie, not tasting it. There was no reason to think Steve would physically bully her. On the surface he was the perfect gentleman, yet she suspected that the civilized exterior only thinly disguised something much more elemental. There was a watchful animosity in him that he showed only to her.

Steve had been to all intents and purposes Magnus's foster son. Jealousy was probably a natural emotion, although even when she'd first arrived she'd thought that at twenty-three he was a bit old to be showing it so blatantly.

She'd certainly have expected him to have outgrown that by now, yet instead he seemed more determined than ever to dislike her—and to find some reason get rid of her.

Well, he wouldn't find that so easy.

Meantime she'd promised they'd try to get along. Turning to him, she gave him her most dazzling smile, before bringing her mind to bear on the conversation and joining in. At least she needn't worry that he'd be too susceptible. The idea almost made her laugh aloud. Sardonically.

Chapter Five

For some weeks there was a sort of truce. Steve and Triss gave every appearance of amicability whenever they were thrown together. There were a few outbursts of temper or frustration from the boys, and when a tense situation developed between one of them and a tutor, Triss intervened, summoning all the tact and mediation skills she'd learned in years of dealing with volatile young men and their older teachers.

"Why didn't you tell me what was going on?" Steve asked her later, when he found her alone in the gym that had once been a ballroom.

Triss turned to put away the weights she'd been using and wiped a thin film of sweat from her forehead with a small towel. She felt at a disadvantage, dressed in clinging shorts and a loose T-shirt, her cheeks flushed and armpits damp from exercising. "I handled it," she said. "The boy apologized, and the tutor's promised me to be a bit less rigid in future."

"The tutor assumed I knew all about it."

"You were busy, and it was a minor problem. There was no need to bring in the big guns."

"Is that what I am? A big gun?"

"Isn't it how you see yourself?" she mocked. "Gunther?"

He smiled slightly. "And what does that make you?"

"A target," she said flippantly. "Have you contacted your accountant yet?"

His smile disappeared. "He's been looking through the files. Will you object if he comes here when he's finished with them? He may have some questions for you."

"Won't it cost to have him here? If his fees are coming out of the trust—"

"I'm paying his fee."

Triss supposed he could afford to. "In that case it's up to you."

He looked about the big room. A badminton net was rigged across the center. "Do you play?" he asked her, disconcerting her with the abrupt change of subject. Maybe he had the grace to be embarrassed.

"Sometimes," she answered him.

"Feel like a game?"

Was this some kind of olive branch? "Okay," she said cautiously.

It was only a game, but if he was succumbing to a masculine urge to demonstrate his probable superiority, she had a surprise for him. Although Triss had never played until coming to the House, she was quite good. She frequently beat the boys, and as a noncontact sport it gave her an ideal way to join in their leisure activities.

Facing Steve across the net when they began, she

was on her mettle. From the first she thought he was
trying her out, testing her skill and strength. Triss gave
him no quarter and soon had him working hard. A
couple of the students wandered in, and after a short
while half a dozen of them were watching, cheering
when either of the players scored a point.

Triss was ahead, and it was Steve's serve. She
looked across the high net and saw him watching her
with gimlet eyes and a feral smile as he gently bounced
the feathered shuttlecock on his racquet. Then he
tossed and slammed it, skimming it over the net. Triss
dived forward, oblivious to the shouts of approval and
encouragement from the sidelines, concentrating
fiercely on the small white object as she batted it back
to him, all the force of her arm behind the swing.

Never had she wanted so much to win. Her com-
petitive instinct wasn't particularly fierce, but today she
was a killer. Sweat filmed her forehead again and trick-
led between her breasts, and her arms ached. Even her
eyes hurt, she was so determined not to lose her con-
centration for a second.

Steve was ahead now and the boys cheered. He
grinned at them and raised a thumb.

Breathing hard, Triss wiped her hands on her shirt
and gripped her racquet, fixing her eyes on her opponent.

Nothing existed except the slap of the racquets, the
sound of rubber-soled feet hitting the floor, and the
swift flight of the shuttlecock between her and the
lynx-eyed man who returned her every shot with swift,
accurate countershots, his long strides taking him to
every corner of the court.

Then when he was close to the net she slammed the
shuttlecock into the far corner. With no hope of reach-

ing it, Steve raised a hand in salute, for once with a hint of respect on his face, and she couldn't help a wide smile of triumph while the boys hooted and clapped.

She finally managed a narrow victory, and the bunch of spectators surged around her, slapping her hand and giving her pats of congratulation.

Steve shouldered through them. Close up she could see he was sweating, too, and his chest heaved. He offered her his hand. "Great game. Congratulations."

"Thanks." Sportsmanship. That's what they tried to teach the students. She let her hand be enveloped in his. "It was close."

"Maybe I'll demand a rematch sometime." His fingers, warm and with a tensile strength, released hers.

Triss was desperately trying to even out her breath. She needed a shower. "Sure," she said, wondering if she could go through that again but not about to say so.

The accountant spent hours talking with Steve, asked a few questions of Triss and left before dinner.

After the meal Steve approached her, his face giving nothing away as he said in a low voice, "Can we talk?"

Triss looked about, checking that everything was under control.

She shrugged, reminding herself she had nothing to fear. "All right."

He led her to Magnus's study, opening the door to usher her in before switching on the light.

The reports were neatly stacked on the desk. Triss went over and idly flipped through the topmost one, then turned to face Steve. "Well?" she challenged him. "What did your expert say?"

Steve had taken only a couple of steps into the room. "There was a discrepancy."

"What?" Triss stiffened.

"Ten dollars in the wrong column." Steve's lips curved wryly, then straightened. "Otherwise he said the accounts were impeccable."

Triss leaned back on the desk, folding her arms. "You must be disappointed."

A muscle moved in his cheek. "But there've been some poor financial decisions made."

When she'd first taken over the accounting she had tried to rationalize the way Magnus operated, appalled that he simply dipped into his private funds whenever there was a shortfall, or relied on erratic donations. She had persuaded him to put aside regular sums for repairs and maintenance and day-to-day expenses, and she'd questioned expenditures that seemed to her unnecessary, unwise, or better deferred, but he had never really understood that a time might come when the money would run out.

Steve said, "You seem to have relied heavily on investment funds for income, but the returns have been…uneven."

"Magnus preferred to invest in creative endeavors."

"Creative endeavors tend to be high risk."

Was that why Steve had given away the artistic side of his education in favor of making money?

Interrupting her wayward thought, he said, "I understood you were in charge of the financial side."

"I kept the books but…" Exasperatingly, Magnus had told everyone proudly that she took care of the finances, while all too often brushing aside her advice.

"It was his money, after all. When he set up the House the market was on an upward spiral. Some of the investments did extremely well...fortunately. But there's been a recession. A couple of companies he—we...put a lot of money into went belly up."

"So overall income has been declining year by year."

"When we needed funds he'd sell off some investments or find someone to make a substantial donation. Old boys who'd done well or a businessman with money to spare. One way or another it always worked."

She looked down at the worn carpet, and had to blink to clear her eyes. No one else had Magnus's unique gift for persuading corporate giants and wealthy tycoons into philanthropy.

Perhaps he had reluctantly come to realize that the House needed drastic financial help, and had left his will intact because he'd hoped Steve's considerable business skills might be turned to saving his mentor's dream.

He would never have admitted he was wrong about Steve's preferred direction in life, but he'd always been quite ruthless in exploiting every avenue for the good of Kurakaha.

Steve walked past the desk and stood looking out of the window behind it. A group of students loped by, jostling and laughing.

Standing up, Triss said to his square-shouldered back, "That draft budget I gave you...have you time to discuss it now?"

It was a moment before he turned. "Guess we'd better."

In her office, she handed him a printout while she

studied the figures on the computer, but after a while Steve drew his chair close to hers where he could point out on the screen what he was referring to.

The tiny shiver over her skin that his proximity evoked made Triss lose focus for a moment, and she had to force herself to concentrate. Once, as he leaned over to run a finger down a column of figures, his other arm rested on the back of her chair, warm behind her shoulders. She felt his breath on her cheek before he sat back rather abruptly, dropping his arm, and returned to studying his paper copy.

Triss drew a quick breath and unclenched her teeth to say, "Yes, you're right, but…" and went on to explain the figures.

His questions were penetrating, his suggestions intelligent. If she told him she'd already considered and discarded something, he listened to her reasoning without comment.

It seemed he'd decided to put aside his prejudice, and after they'd finished, Triss felt better than she had since Magnus's death.

Steve straightened in his chair, stretched and got up.

Hands thrust into his pockets, he took a few paces from the desk before turning to face her. "Magnus left you everything that wasn't tied to the House."

Triss just stopped herself from making a grimace. "Yes," she said warily.

He hesitated, as if uncertain how to word his next question. "So, *did* he provide adequately for his widow?"

"Yes." Triss clamped her lips tightly shut. She wasn't going to tell him how meager that provision had actually turned out to be. It was irrelevant anyway.

When she didn't elaborate he said, "Hasn't your accountant made any comment on the financial situation of the House?''

''Several times he recommended shifting some money into more secure investments. But that's a long-term strategy.''

''And we need an injection of cash in the short term. I can provide that. But pouring money in without setting up a source of continuing income won't keep the trust going indefinitely.''

''I know that.'' If only Magnus had realized it.

Steve gave her a half smile. ''We just agreed on something.''

''So we did.'' Triss flexed her shoulders, and stifled a yawn with her hand. She'd been working long hours, trying to come up with a budget that wouldn't stretch the available and projected resources too far, and the extra stress of waiting for Steve's accountant to give his verdict hadn't helped her to sleep when she did get to bed.

''You're tired,'' Steve diagnosed brilliantly. ''Maybe we should quit while we're ahead.''

Triss could only concur with that. She closed down the computer and stood up. Steve went to the door to open it for her.

And as he had once before, he paused with his hand on the knob, and automatically her defenses began to gather, her spine tingling and a knot forming in her stomach. Only this time, instead of repeating the insolent, encompassing stare he'd assailed her with the day of her husband's funeral, he kept his eyes on her face, giving her a penetrating look that she found difficult to read. As if he was searching for something.

But she wasn't ready to let Gunther Stevens plumb the depths of her soul. Their tentative, unspoken truce was too new and fragile for such intimacy. Deliberately she swept her lashes down, hiding her eyes.

The moment stretched. She could feel the blood running through her veins, the hurried beat of a tiny pulse in her temple. Fascinated, she watched Steve's knuckles whiten as his hand tightened on the china doorknob. He made a low sound, a cut-off, reluctant grunt, and wrenched open the door, his breath audibly leaving his chest.

Triss took a step forward, then turned in the doorway, daring to look at him. His face was set in concrete-hard lines, his mouth a stern slash, and his eyes burned darkly.

"Steve?" Moved by a compulsion to offer some kind of understanding, although she was unsure of what, Triss raised a hand to his arm.

He jerked out of her reach. "Don't touch me." His voice grated.

Triss let her hand fall. Something in her throat obstructed speech. She took a hasty step back, shook her head in bewilderment and fled.

What was that about? she asked herself minutes later, leaning back against the closed door of her own flat, her arms defensively crossed over her breasts. He couldn't even stand her to touch him? He hated her that much? Or...

Another, fantastic answer presented itself, and she said aloud, "No!"

A sexual element in the unmistakable tension between her and Steve was something she didn't want to face. He'd never liked her and she'd always been wary around him, since her early overtures of friendliness had fallen on the stony ground of his studied indifference.

Later the indifference had turned to downright animosity that he couldn't—or didn't bother to—hide from Magnus.

Triss's chief emotion at the time of Steve's leaving had been guilty relief. The atmosphere was considerably less strained but she was aware of Magnus's furious disappointment and, however irrationally, felt she was partly responsible for the estrangement.

Although Steve had kept up a sporadic correspondence, and yearly an increasingly generous donation arrived toward the upkeep of the House, the rift had never really healed.

Pushing away from the door, she unwrapped her arms from about herself, making for the bathroom.

Maybe sexuality was an unacknowledged part of every interaction between a man and a woman. Some people said so.

She turned on the shower, absently watching it run for a minute or two before she began to undress. Stepping under the warm water, she closed her eyes, trying to blank her mind.

But her body wouldn't cooperate. Her breasts felt full and heavy and there was a strange ache in her thighs, spreading upward.

Impatiently she reached out and turned the shower to cold, gasping at the resultant shock.

When she crawled into bed she was still shivering. The sheets were cold, too, with an impersonal disinfected crispness. Twice a week all the sheets and towels from the House were loaded into a truck and exchanged for clean linen from a commercial laundry. It was cheaper than employing staff to do the job.

Triss curled into a defensive fetal position, pulling the covers about her shoulders.

The other side of the bed was empty. There was an emptiness inside her, too. Sex had held a minor place in Magnus's canon of priorities, and making love had been an occasional but pleasant part of their lives. She hadn't expected to miss it much, but right now she longed for a man's arms about her, just to feel a warm masculine body close to hers.

Grabbing a pillow, she hugged it tightly, squeezing her eyes shut. But the tears wouldn't be stopped this time. They stung at her eyes and burned down her cheeks, and in the end she gave in and let them flow, her face buried in the cool cotton pillow slip, her sobs stifled by the softness inside it.

Afterward she slept as she hadn't slept in months.

In the morning she felt sluggish and her eyelids were swollen. She took a horrified glance at herself in the bathroom mirror and decided to skip breakfast in the dining room.

Instead she shook out ice cubes from the tray in the tiny fridge installed in the flat, and spent half an hour applying them in the hope of hiding the evidence of her crying jag.

Because it was Saturday she dressed in comfortable cotton pants and a white shirt, and was carefully applying a disguising blue eye shadow when there was a knock on the door.

Triss finished stroking the tiny brush over her lids, put it down and went to the door, pushing back her hair behind her ears. She really must get it cut, or start fastening it out of the way.

Steve stood there, in jeans and a casual shirt. His eyes made a lightning inspection of her, and she realized she hadn't put on her shoes. She seldom wore heels higher than a couple of inches, but in her bare feet the difference in their heights was emphasized.

His gaze returning to her face, Steve said, "We wondered why you weren't at breakfast. I volunteered to investigate."

"I slept in." She avoided looking at him. "I'm not very hungry. Thanks for checking."

She made to close the door but he stopped it. "Are you all right?" He lifted a hand and briefly laid the backs of his fingers against her cheek, then immediately withdrew as though he'd done it without thinking. "You look as if you might have a bit of fever."

"I don't. I'm fine." She stepped back involuntarily at the touch of his hand and, apparently misinterpreting the movement as an invitation, he followed, his eyes searching.

Made uncomfortable by his scrutiny, she wheeled away, fetching up a few feet from him before she swung about and faced him.

"So what's wrong?" he asked.

"Nothing!" Triss answered sharply. "Nothing that hasn't been wrong ever since…"

Since Magnus died—even since her parents died. This latest bereavement had brought back all the misery and anguish she'd suffered then. That she should have got over years ago.

She swallowed hard, and turned from him again, gritting her teeth. "You can tell everyone I'm perfectly all right."

"I'm not in the habit of telling lies."

"It's not a lie."

"How long since you took a day off?"

"What?" The question made her look at him again.

"Zed and Hana said you've hardly left the place

since Magnus died—'' He was regarding her with veiled, slightly surprised concern.

"That's not true—"

"—except to fetch supplies."

"I do my personal shopping at the same time. It saves petrol."

"I'm not talking about shopping. I'm talking about relaxing."

"I relax in the evenings."

"They reckon you're always on duty. They're supposed to take over every second weekend, but lately you've kept telling them not to worry about it."

"Half the boys go home, and Zed and Hana have a family. There's no need for them to stick around when I'm here."

"They think you need a break. Why don't you just take off and let us hold the fort?"

"Take off where?"

"Wherever you like. Visit someone, or see a show of some sort. Go to an art gallery…"

"On my own?" Remembering her loneliness last night, she knew those things would only emphasize her sense of isolation. Her friends—hers and Magnus's— would be all sympathy and concern, and they'd either talk about him or scout uncomfortably round the subject. She wasn't ready for that. And any public place where there were people, she'd stand out as a single among couples and groups. "No, thanks."

Steve was studying her. "Get your shoes," he said. "And a jacket and anything else you need for a day out."

"I told you—"

"You needn't go alone. I'll just have a word with Hana."

He left the door open and disappeared down the stairs, taking them two at a time from the sound of his footsteps.

Maybe he was right—or Zed and Hana were. She had been under stress, and even though some of the strain had eased with Steve's acceptance that she hadn't been cooking the accounts, last night's emotional storm had left her feeling curiously empty and listless.

Presumably Steve was asking Hana if she would be Triss's companion for the day.

She liked Hana, but they had few interests in common. Hana tended to be wrapped up in her children, and any spare time she could squeeze between her family and her job as cook was spent sewing for them, or in the traditional Maori weaving that was her passion. While Triss admired her skill, she had no aptitude herself for crafts or art. Having taken a business course after leaving high school, she had headed for a career in office work, knowing she wasn't creative. Her attention to detail, her flair for getting things done and a perfectionist attitude had taken her into events organization, where she'd excelled, until Magnus had married her and put her talents to good use at Kura-kaha.

She pulled on a pair of shoes and took a light jacket from its hanger in her wardrobe. After shoving a coin purse and a couple of tissues into the jacket's side pocket, she was closing her outer door when Steve came back up.

"Ready?" He glanced at her with apparent approval, and stood back to let her go first.

At the foot of the stairs she turned to go toward the back of the house and the garage, but he put a hand on her waist, guiding her to the front door. "The car's here."

Not her car, nor Zed and Hana's, but the car that Steve had bought for his own use soon after his arrival. Triss was halfway down the front steps before she realized Hana wasn't inside it.

"Where's…?"

But Steve was opening the passenger door for her, urging her in. He closed it behind her and went round the front, then slid into the driver's seat. While Triss was catching her breath and readjusting her mind, he put the car in motion and as they glided toward the gate he said, "Where would you like to go?"

Chapter Six

"I don't know." Hearing how indecisive and feeble that sounded, Triss suggested randomly, "A beach?"

"Sure." Steve slowed at the gateway, checking for traffic. "Any particular one?"

"No."

"Right." He accelerated onto the road. "Leave it to me."

The day was fine and clear but too cool for swimming. Triss wasn't sure why she'd asked for a beach, except that lately the House had seemed a bit claustrophobic, and she fancied a sea breeze and a wide ocean.

Steve said, "If you look in the glove box you'll find a toasted sandwich Hana made for you. And there's a miniflask of coffee on the back seat."

She'd said she wasn't hungry, but the sandwich, wrapped in foil, was still warm, and the smell of cheese and bacon woke her taste buds. The coffee helped too; she began to feel a faint lift of her spirits.

Steve drove for about half an hour, turning onto the

main road and then off it again, eventually starting
down a winding and narrow dirt road, bumping
through an open farm gate and across undulating paddocks of cropped grass.

"Where are we?" Triss asked. She'd been almost
in a trance, not noticing much where they were going,
content for once to allow someone else to make the
decisions. Even though the someone else was Steve.

"On Maori land. The owners are happy to share as
long we don't do any damage or leave litter about. It's
only used by people who know about it. I have the
idea you don't want to be around lots of people."

He stopped the car beside two others, above an uneven line of overshadowing pohutukawa trees, their
thick, twisted trunks peeling, the silver-backed leaves
turning in a restless breeze. White-crested breakers
rushed untidily to a shingly gray shore.

Steve climbed out and Triss followed, lifting her
face to the cool wind that blew her hair cleanly back
and made her eyes half close.

While Steve locked the doors she went to the ragged
edge where tough buffalo grass ended at a shallow
bank of sand.

She was already making her way down when he
joined her on the crunchy shingle mixed with wave-
ground white shells.

Nearer the water, the shingle gave way to smooth,
dun-colored sand. Once they reached it they slipped
off their shoes and rolled their trousers above their ankles, allowing the shallow wavelets to lap about their
feet.

A lone fisherman wielded a rod from a pile of shining black rocks that bounded the beach, but the occu-
pants of the other car were nowhere to be seen.

Triss stooped to pick up a purple scallop shell, no bigger than her thumbnail, and slipped it into her pocket.

The boom and hiss of the waves was soothing, and the salty breeze exhilarating—a curious contrast, like the man who walked silently at her side, allowing her to set the pace. His presence was a bulwark against loneliness, and yet she was acutely aware of the humming along her nerves that he evoked.

Refusing to think about that, she lifted her face to the wind, watching a few scudding clouds being slowly torn to white rags. Her foot caught against a smooth hump of driftwood half-buried in the sand, and she stumbled.

Steve caught her arm, steadying her.

She turned toward him with a smile, pushing windblown hair from her eyes. "Thanks."

His face had a peculiar tightness about it, and his eyes, a stormy gray, held disturbing intentness before he released her and they walked on.

Triss experienced a strange emotion—part fear, part dismay and part guilty excitement. She took in a deep gulp of pungent sea air.

She wouldn't think about it. Today was meant to help her relax, to stop thinking and worrying…and grieving. For the first time the leaden weight that had oppressed her had begun to lift.

Life goes on. The old cliché came unbidden into her mind. Today she felt truly alive. She could hardly remember the last time that had been true.

Picking up a weathered, twisted stick that lay on the sand, she hurled it as far as she could into the waves, watching it bob and twirl as it was carried farther and farther from the shore.

Steve halted beside her, his shirt rippling in the breeze. "Better?" he asked.

"Yes."

He bent, scooping a small, flat stone into his fingers, and threw it after the stick. The stone skipped twice along the smoother water beyond an incoming crest, and then sank.

"Oh, clever!" Triss mocked.

Steve shook his head. "I used to be able to skip them half a dozen times."

They resumed walking and lapsed back into silence until they reached the rocks, where a narrow passageway of sand wound between rough, dark boulders.

"There's a cove through there," Steve said, "if you want to go farther."

"Let's."

Triss went first, splashing through shallow pools where colonies of blue and orange starfish clung to the rocky sides, and hermit crabs sidled out of the way. She felt almost like a child again, playing in the water, enjoying the sun and the wind and the smell of the sea. She stopped and for no reason at all shook back her hair and raised her face to the blue, cloud-streaked sky, catching Steve's eyes on her and sending him a smile of pure bliss before moving on.

"Careful," Steve warned when a deeper pool barred the way, but Triss had always been surefooted and she negotiated her way easily from one slippery rock to another.

After clambering precariously over larger rocks, avoiding the sharp-shelled bunches of black baby mussels that clung to them, she jumped onto soft, sun-warmed sand, turning as Steve followed.

"It's lovely!" she said, looking about them. The

cove was very small, the sand sloping from the water up to an overhanging cliff that hung like a pale curtain, with orange-flowered flax and creamy toe-toe feathers trembling in the breeze at the top. A few stray plants clung to the rock face, and at its base a shallow scoop made a perfect place to sit on the sand and admire the sea.

Triss sat down and leaned on the smooth sandstone. Steve watched her with a slight smile on his lips, looking a little bemused, then wandered to the edge of the water and found another stone. This one skipped three times, and Triss ironically applauded.

He came toward her, grinning, and she squinted at him against the sun, raising a hand to shade her eyes. He flopped down on the sand, almost at right angles to her, long legs stretched before him, one bare ankle resting over the other. Crossing his arms, he rested his head on the wall of rock behind him and closed his eyes.

He too had been under stress lately. It couldn't have been easy, rearranging his life and moving from one country to another. And while Triss had lost her husband, he had lost the man he admitted had changed his life, the nearest thing he'd had to a father.

For the past few years, an estranged father. Whom he'd never had a chance to say goodbye to.

Steve turned his head to look at her, as if he'd felt her gaze. "What are you thinking about?" he asked her.

"I was thinking how you must have felt—when Magnus died."

"It's over now."

Grief was never over. She knew that from experience. Time healed but the scars remained, still sensitive to reminder. "He loved you," she said, "as much as he loved anyone."

Steve seemed to go very still. "Are you saying he didn't love *you*?"

Startled at the blunt question, Triss shook her head. She looked away from him, drawing a circular pattern with her finger in the sand. "No, of course I'm not saying that."

Steve got up abruptly and walked diagonally across the sand, as though he needed to get as far away from her as possible.

Perplexed, Triss stared after him, watching him thrust his hands into the back pockets of his jeans, tilt his head so that the wind lifted his hair from his forehead and then stand rock still, feet apart, his shoulders braced.

Maybe they would get on better now, Triss thought hopefully. They should have been helping each other find shared comfort in their mutual loss instead of conducting some low-key private war. But perhaps that was over now that Steve knew she had been honest in her dealings with the money for the House.

The sun dazzled off the water, making her eyes hurt. A rogue wave swept farther up the shore than all the others, swirling foam about Steve's ankles, but he didn't move. Suddenly extremely tired, Triss slid down on the sand, letting her head rest on its softness, uncaring that it would get into her hair. She could shower it out later.

The sky was a brilliant, hurting blue. High up, a seagull lazed across her vision, wings spread and still, then a couple of languid flaps took it beyond the cliff top and it disappeared. Faintly she could hear the rattle of the broad, stiff flax leaves on the cliff edge, worried by the wind. Her eyes closed.

When she opened them the sun had moved and the shadow of the cliff lay over her face. Steve had returned and was sitting where he had before, one arm resting on a raised knee as he watched her.

"Have a good sleep?" he asked her.

Embarrassed, she struggled to sit up. The sea and sky coalesced momentarily, then steadied. She brushed sand from her hair with her fingers. "Sorry."

"What for? I didn't bring you here to entertain me. You probably needed that."

"I have some sleep to catch up on." Obviously last night hadn't been enough.

Steve nodded. "The tide's come in so we're stuck here for a while, unless you want to risk climbing the cliff. I wouldn't advise it."

"You should have woken me!"

He shook his head. "No hurry. I hope you're not hungry though. Hana and I threw a picnic together for us but it's in the car."

"I'm not hungry. What about you?"

"I had a decent breakfast."

"So did I…and later than yours."

He looked away from her to the onrushing tide, his eyes narrowed against the glare. "I didn't realize I was missing all this," he said, "the last few years."

"Not until you came home?"

Steve looked at her again. "The concept's never meant much to me."

Triss drew up her knees and wrapped her arms about them. "Maybe you needed to go away to learn to appreciate it."

The slight movement of his head might have indicated agreement. "Where do you call home?" he asked. "You're Australian, aren't you?"

Magnus had met her in Australia. He'd been invited to give a guest lecture at a prestigious international music seminar, and while there he had taken the opportunity to drum up financial support for the school and spread the word about his talented students who might be looking for jobs or further education outside New Zealand.

"I was born here," Triss said. "My parents moved to Australia when I was five."

"You wouldn't remember much."

"No, but I used to dream sometimes about a huge, wide beach with dark sand covered in patterns of ripples, and enormous black cliffs that had caves in them. White water as far as the eye could see, except under the curves of the breakers—you know how it turns smooth and green there, like liquid glass. I've never found that place, but I'm sure it was a New Zealand beach."

"One you'd visited before you went away?"

"I guess so."

He was studying her as if weighing his next question. "Do you want to go back to Australia now?"

Triss picked up a handful of sand and let it trickle through her fingers, watching the tiny veil fall and spread and merge with the rest of the beach. "Is that what you'd like me to do? Go away and leave Kurakaha to you?"

"It's what you suggested I should do."

"Yes, I did." She tipped the last gritty grains from her palm and dusted her hands together. "And you would have liked to get rid of me."

"Past tense," he said succinctly.

That cautious fluttering in her chest might have been hope. Hugging her knees again, she said, "I don't have any ties in Australia. A few friends I keep in touch with—via Christmas cards, an occasional letter or e-mail. My parents are gone." And the home they had made for her, because she'd been too young to live alone.

"I know. An accident, wasn't it?"

"They were in a tour boat on a river, having a holiday to celebrate twenty years of marriage. The boat hit something and overturned. Neither of them made it to shore."

After a short silence Steve said slowly, "How old were you?"

"Fifteen."

"Do you have other family?" Steve asked after a moment.

"One uncle. He took me to live with him in Darwin. I didn't want to leave my home and friends, but I had no choice."

"That must have been rough for a girl. Was he married?"

"Divorced. He didn't know what to do with a teenage girl, too young to fend for myself, too old to need a nanny or a baby-sitter. He did his best but…I missed my father and mother. I'm sure he was relieved when I was off his hands and earning a living."

"Do you keep in touch?"

"Oh, yes. He checks on me occasionally, we write…"

"He didn't come to Magnus's funeral?"

"Too far. And there wasn't time."

Steve had come though. Even when he was unaware of the contents of Magnus's will. "Do you feel trapped,'' she asked him, ''being made responsible for the House?'' It had made a huge difference to his life-style. She wouldn't have been surprised if he resented the unasked-for burden.

He said slowly, ''I owe it to Magnus. If it's what he wanted... What about you? I thought—''

When he stopped there Triss finished for him. ''You thought I'd want to take off as soon as I could.''

Steve hunched one shoulder and let it fall. ''You haven't.''

''You're not the only one with a sense of... responsibility.'' Or duty, or obligation, whatever he liked to call it. ''Magnus would have wanted me to keep the House running.''

''That's your forte, isn't it? Organization. Your office is a model.''

She looked sideways at him to gauge if he was being snide, but he looked thoughtful, curious.

''After my parents died,'' she confessed, ''I felt as if the world was out of control, nothing was in its proper place...and I needed to make it right again. I guess that sounds silly.''

''No. I felt like that for most of my life. Why do you think I chose making machines over making music? I looked at all those dedicated musicians and saw how few can make a decent, regular income. Before I was fifteen I'd had a gutful of living hand to mouth, and not having control of my own life. I wanted to make money—real money—because it's a guarantee of freedom.''

''Then maybe you can understand—for a while I became obsessive about order...a place for everything and everything in its place. I checked on every little detail of every single thing I did. Subconsciously I suppose I thought I could stave off fate by leaving nothing to chance. By the time I realized what I was doing it had become a habit. Then I made an effort to relax a bit, because I think I was close to needing counseling, but the habit was an asset when I applied for a job as an events organizer.'' She'd found her niche and had enjoyed the constant challenges thrown at her to ensure every project ran without a hitch. "And at Kurakaha," she added.

Steve turned to stare at the ocean view, ran a hand over his hair and then looked back at her. "You've done a good job at the House, under difficulties. I apologize," he said quietly, "if I've been unfair."

It didn't seem to matter much now. Triss lifted a shoulder in acknowledgment. "I suppose you were jealous."

"*Jealous?*" The unexpected lash of his voice made her flinch. His back had gone rigid, his jaw aggressive.

"Magnus was your father figure. You were close."

He said bluntly, "I never thought of him as my *father.*" Then he gave a strange little laugh. "Did you?"

"I knew he'd sort of adopted you."

"That isn't what I meant." Steve moved restlessly and looked at the water again, as if willing it to recede, but it was still creeping up the beach.

Triss said, "How high will it get?"

"Don't worry." Steve turned to her again. "Except in a storm, it only comes halfway up the sand." As if he'd made a deliberate decision, he stretched out his legs again and relaxed.

Triss said, "Do you ever regret giving up your music?"

His eyes half-closed, he moved his head in negation.

"I haven't. Just put it to a different use. I couldn't make the instruments I do without the knowledge of music that Magnus gave me. It wasn't the waste that he thought it was. I play when the mood takes me, but not for money or acclaim. And I listen a lot to the music of the world, because I want to enable musicians to reproduce it."

"The music of the world?"

"There's music all around us. Can't you hear it?"

"The sea, the wind?" A raucous screech from overhead made her raise her eyes to a couple of gulls dipping and twirling against the sky. "That?"

Steve's eyes gleamed with humor. "That, too. If you listen hard you can hear the sand shifting."

Triss cast him a skeptical look. For several minutes she listened, and almost imagined she could discern the whisper of tiny grains moving against each other as the breeze skimmed across the sand.

"Hear it?" Steve asked.

Triss laughed. "Inaudible to the human ear."

"You don't have to hear it with your ears."

"Then yes," she admitted, "I hear it."

Something passed between them without words—a moment of communication. A salt-laden gust of wind blowing her hair into her eyes broke the brief spell. She shook her head back and lifted a hand to finger the fine tresses away. "I really have to get a haircut."

"Don't. It's beautiful."

Triss stared, then laughed uncertainly. "It's a nuisance."

Steve looked away as though he regretted his comment.

"But thank you, anyway."

He didn't seem to be listening.

"How long before we can get back to the car?" she asked him.

Glancing at her, he said, "Bored already? You wanted a beach—" he waved a hand at it "—you've got one."

"I'm not bored. The water's very…restful."

He gave her a keen look. "But not the company?"

"The company's…interesting."

He inclined his head. "If you want me to shut up or go away, say so. This is your day off."

Ostentatiously she looked about them. "Where would you go?"

"Not far. Are you afraid of being left?"

"Yes," she said, surprising herself more than him, she suspected. Usually quite self-sufficient, suddenly she needed someone around. At least for this short while. "I haven't got used to being alone yet." Magnus had helped fill the emptiness inside her, but he was gone. For the second time in her life she felt abandoned, wandering in the dark alone.

Steve's face changed, the hard angles altering in some subtle way. He reached out a hand and took one of hers. "You're not alone." His strong fingers closed about hers.

"Neither are you," she said involuntarily.

Steve looked a little startled, then his mouth moved in a faint smile. He nodded, and gazed down at their joined hands.

For a long time they sat there, talking desultorily, but mostly in silence. Slowly Triss's tension drained away, replaced by a pleasant lethargy. She was almost sorry when the waves had receded far enough for them to retrace their path back to the car.

Steve opened the luggage compartment and brought

out a large plastic container and a plaid tablecloth. ''Shall we eat here?'' he suggested.

Triss spread the cloth on the grass and he opened the container to reveal bread rolls, a pot of margarine, ham slices and the makings of salad sandwiches, along with biscuits, fruit and canned juice.

A party of wet-suited teenagers arrived in a station wagon, untied surf boards from the top of the vehicle and went noisily down to the waves. Later a young couple with two small children appeared from the beach and drove away. The children waved at Triss and Steve from the back of the car, and they waved back.

Steve lay on the grass, his hands folded under his head. ''Do you want to go somewhere else?'' he asked.

''I'm happy to stay here.''

''Good.'' He closed his eyes and in a few minutes she was almost sure he was asleep. She inspected his face, the strong brows and jutting nose, the firm mouth softened in sleep, lips slightly parted. His chest rose and fell evenly.

She'd seen a side of him today that he'd never shown her before. Thoughtful, sympathetic, gentle.

Gentleness was the last thing she would have associated with Steve.

His lids fluttered and she looked hastily away, but when he didn't move she glanced back at him, and his eyes were still shut. A striped fly buzzed by and landed on his forehead, causing it to furrow, but he didn't try to brush it away. Triss leaned over and waved at the intruder, chasing it off. This close, she could see the tiny creases near Steve's eyes, and a trace of dampness along his hairline. His cheeks were slightly beard-shadowed already, and she caught herself wondering how they would feel against her skin.

Jerking upright, she mentally shook herself, appalled at the trend of her thoughts, and scrambled to her feet.

She backed away, then slid down the bank to the beach and started across the sand. At the edge of the waves she splashed in calf deep, bending to scoop water into her hand and splash it over her heated face.

A wave raced in and soaked the bottoms of her rolled-up trousers before she stepped back. The taste of bitter salt was on her lips, and when she turned to walk along the beach her wet trousers felt clammy against her skin. She concentrated on those sensations.

Triss had never thought of herself as a particularly highly sexed person. Sex wasn't love, it was no substitute for emotional closeness, and although she liked it well enough, experience led her to believe that the whole business had been overrated.

Maybe her body was trying to tell her something. She was still a young woman, widowed, presumably fertile, and nature was impatient.

Until very recently Steve had been frankly hostile, suspecting her of God knew what. And today, just because he'd been kind and conciliatory, she was frighteningly close to completely letting down her guard, allowing his undoubted male attraction to lead her into a dangerous temptation.

Right now she was emotionally vulnerable, that was it. She could imagine what Steve would think if she threw herself at him, if she'd leaned down as she'd momentarily wanted to do and woken him with a kiss.

He'd go right back to despising her. And with reason.

She picked up a pretty spiral shell, found it was broken and tossed it into the waves.

On her return, Steve was leaning on the front of the car, his hands in his pockets. He watched her approach, and when she slipped on the crumbling bank and grasped a tuft of grass to help, he stepped forward and gripped her wrist, hauling her up.

"Thanks," she said. "Sorry if you've been waiting."

"No problem. Are you okay?"

"Yes." She shot him a fleeting glance. "Did you have a nice nap?"

"I didn't mean to go to sleep."

Triss tried to wipe sand from her feet on the springy grass. "There's something about the sea air, isn't there?" she said.

"And good food." He reached into the back of the car and emerged with a small towel. Opening the passenger door, he said, "Here," and guided her into the seat so that she sat sideways.

He knelt on the grass and lifted her foot to his knee, wiping away sand with the towel.

"I can do that." She reached out for the towel. The warmth of his thigh through the material of his jeans, the feel of his fingers working the towel over her foot, were too disturbing.

Steve looked up, met her eyes with his, then handed her the towel and got to his feet. He strolled to the bank and stood with his back to her while she finished and slipped on her shoes.

"Thank you," she said, and when he turned gave him back the towel.

"How would you like to have dinner out? If we're playing hooky we might as well do it properly."

"I'm not dressed for that." Her trousers would dry but they'd hardly pass muster in a fine dining establishment.

He looked her over critically. "So it'll have to be a restaurant where they don't mind casual dress. I'm sure we can find some place."

"What about Hana and Zed? They'll expect us—"

"I told them not to worry if we weren't in for the evening meal."

As she still hesitated he said, "It's entirely your choice."

Hana's cooking was very good, but of necessity meals prepared for a crowd lacked the individuality of taste and presentation that a good restaurant could provide. It was a long time since Triss had eaten out. "All right," she said.

Steve drove into the city and took a while to find a decent looking place that wouldn't frown on their windswept appearance and crumpled casual attire, but eventually they were welcomed to a seafood restaurant on the harborfront, hung with fishing nets and floats and furnished with bare wooden tables.

It was still early and the maître d' suggested a drink in the small bar before they ate.

"I'll pay for mine," Triss said.

As she took her purse from her pocket Steve's hand firmly closed over hers. "Put that away."

"I can't let you—"

"I won't let *you*."

"You know you're being a male chauvinist?"

"I also know that overall men are still paid better than women."

"Where did you hear that?"

"Read it in the paper. Didn't you?"

"Yes...but—"

"So it's only fair that a man who invites a woman to dinner should pay for the pleasure of her company."

"I'm not sure I like you putting it that way. It sounds a bit like..."

"I wouldn't take that thought any further if I were you." The skin about his eyes creased as he killed a smile. "What do you want to drink?"

Chapter Seven

Triss gave up. "I thought," she confessed over the drink he'd bought her, "you'd be all for the superiority of men."

"Why would you think that?"

Maybe she was being unfair to make that assumption on the basis of his distrust of her. She decided not to go there. "I suppose because you open doors and pull out chairs for women. It's old-fashioned…but kind of nice," she added quickly.

"That foster mother I told you about," he said. "She was old-fashioned, I suppose. But I haven't forgotten what she'd taught me. I guess it's a tribute to her memory." His eyes darkened and he swirled the remains of the drink in his glass and tossed the wine down his throat.

"Her memory? You don't know if she…?"

"She died. Not then, later. I looked her up a few years back. A whim."

"I'm sorry. You were fond of her."

"I respected her."

The correction was a little chilling. "You don't respect many women, do you?" She twirled her own glass between her fingers.

"Not many have given me reason to."

"That's a jaundiced view of an entire sex! Half the population?"

"There aren't a lot of men I respect either." His mocking glance challenged her.

"Maybe you expect too much."

He regarded her silently. "Possibly. My favorite foster mother and...your husband...set very high standards."

And he had decided to follow their example. It was difficult to find fault with that. "High standards aren't always easy to live up to." She lifted her glass and finished her wine.

"I guess not." He was gazing at her with an unreadable expression. "Do you want another drink?"

"No, thanks. What about you?"

"Not if I'm driving you home."

If? Triss looked up quickly, but there was nothing in his face to suggest any hidden meaning. Of course he hadn't been obliquely propositioning her!

Ashamed of her suspicion, she looked away again, her cheeks uncomfortably warm, and ran her tongue over dry lips.

Steve shifted, drawing her eyes again. He was leaning back, surveying her from beneath lowered lids, so that she couldn't see the expression in his eyes, but his mouth had a downward curve at one corner.

Triss was relieved that the waiter came to conduct them to a table then, and she sprang up to follow the man across the room.

They were not late getting back. A few of the boys kicking a ball around near the garage scattered out of the way. Their greeting hoots and whistles were silenced by Steve as he got out and opened Triss's door before garaging the car. "Okay, guys," he said with his usual easy authority. "Cut it out."

They did, and Triss was grateful. "Thank you, I've had a nice day," she murmured quickly to Steve, then said good-night to the boys and hurried into the house.

Zed was watching TV with a few of the other students. She paused in the doorway to tell him she was back and he could go home.

The big man ambled to the door. "You look better," he informed her. "Done you good to get away."

"Thanks for holding the fort. And please tell Hana the toasted sandwich and the picnic were both great."

"I'll tell her. You getting on better with Steve? He's a good guy, you know."

"Yes," she said, answering both questions. The trouble was, he'd never believed she was a good woman.

Maybe that had changed. Triss fervently hoped so.

She had hardly time to find out, because the following day Steve came into her office and said, "I need to go back to L.A. for a few weeks."

"Something wrong?" she asked. He seemed put out.

"I wasn't expecting to have to leave so soon, but there's been a hitch about delivery of a massive order and I need to sort things out. You wanted us to go over the list of prospective tutors for next year. Can we do that today?''

Mentally rearranging her priorities, Triss thought for a moment. ''Yes. When do you leave?''

''The first flight I can get on tomorrow. Sorry about this.''

''I'll book it for you if you like.''

''Thanks.'' Steve looked surprised.

Triss turned to the computer. ''Sit down,'' she said, pulling open a drawer and placing a thin folder on the desk. ''This is the list of candidates.''

Steve began flipping through it while she dialed into the Internet, and a few minutes later she printed out a sheet of paper and handed it to him.

''Pick up your boarding pass at the airport counter,'' she said.

He glanced at the paper, folded it and slipped it into his pocket. ''You're very efficient.''

''Why do you think Magnus married me?''

The arrested look in his eyes made her flush. ''Joke,'' she said with desperate flippancy.

''Magnus was crazy about you.'' His voice sounded strange, rasping. ''He must have been.''

Because he'd married her? Triss found she couldn't meet Steve's eyes, afraid of what she might see in them. He had never thought her worthy of being Magnus's wife. Maybe yesterday hadn't changed everything after all.

Unnecessarily, she straightened a small pile of papers, aligning the edges.

No matter what Steve thought, it had been her efficiency that had first drawn Magnus's attention.

He had sought her out to congratulate her on the

smooth running of the music seminar he'd attended, and when he invited her to dine with him, it was to persuade her to come to New Zealand and take charge of arrangements for a festival of which he was a planning committee member.

With nothing to hold her in Australia, she'd jumped at the chance and had pulled out all the stops to make the festival a success.

After it was over he'd invited her to accompany him to a gala opera event, she supposed as a kind of reward.

Wanting to live up to his reputation, she had invested in a new dress and an expensive pair of elegant shoes—medium-heeled because she was almost as tall as Magnus—and had her hair specially styled for the occasion.

Admiring glances directed at her by other men, and mildly envious or frankly incredulous ones directed at him, had their effect. By the end of the evening he had a proprietorial hand at her waist and was standing taller, prouder.

Triss had been touched that this immensely clever and charismatic man found her presence at his side a boost to his self-esteem. Later he asked her permission before kissing her good-night, and she'd kissed him back warmly in return. She'd had a nice evening and she wanted him to know it. When he asked her out again, she accepted with scarcely a hesitation.

Magnus had introduced her to the inner circle of music and art, and taught her more about them in six weeks than she'd learned in her twenty-three years.

He never asked for more than a kiss at the end of their dates, and his proposal had come as a surprise. Not that she had any regrets. It had been a successful and fulfilling partnership despite the disparity in their ages and the difference in their talents. Her intense practicality and passion for order were a perfect foil for Magnus's visionary, artistic personality; he had respected her abilities and she had never lost her admiration for him. She hadn't been unhappy.

"This is a pretty impressive list," Steve said.

"Kurakaha has a pretty impressive reputation. Each year now we get expressions of interest from people hoping to take part in our short special programs."

"Have all these expressed interest?" Steve asked.

"No. But some are just beginning their careers and will probably love to do it. The more established ones could need some persuasion."

"There are no women's names here." Steve looked up.

"You know how Magnus felt." That boys needed strong male role models and firm handling. In retrospect, she shouldn't have been surprised that he had stubbornly clung to the will that had brought Steve back to provide that.

"He brought *you* here, and there's Hana."

"Wives. Women tutors would alter the character of the place, although I've sometimes thought…"

"That it needed altering?" Steve picked up quickly.

"He trusted us!"

"To keep the place going. He didn't stipulate we weren't to make any changes. A few women tutors won't overturn everything, Triss."

Just hearing him say her name affected her with a kind of pleasurable shock that she couldn't control. He so seldom used it. Triss closed her lips.

Steve looked at her thoughtfully. "Think about it."

"I will," she promised, torn between loyalty to Magnus and her own feeling that Steve was right.

Triss would never have believed she would miss Steve while he was away. He had become part of the life of the House in a manner she hadn't fully appreciated, in minor but significant ways quietly taking some of the burden of running the place from her shoulders, so subtly that she had scarcely even noticed.

She sent him e-mail reports and a revised list of suggested tutors. After ten days he phoned her, his deep voice as clear as if he were in the next room. She pictured him relaxing on a hotel bed somewhere, the collar of his shirt undone and his dark head resting against a couple of pillows. "How are the plans going for next year?" he asked her.

Making her own voice crisp, she reported on the replies she'd received so far to several letters.

"Uh-huh."

She had the feeling he wasn't really concentrating. "It's slow, though," she worried. "I was thinking maybe you might be able to see some of them face-to-face and talk them into coming."

He gave a soft laugh. "Why me? You might have more success. An attractive woman—"

Triss took a deep breath. "You're forgetting," she said, "some of those on our new list are female. Maybe you should try batting *your* eyelashes at them. And flex a few of those great muscles of yours while you're about it. I'm sure all the women would fall at your feet."

"Ow." She could hear laughter in his voice. "I've

offended you. I do beg your pardon.'' After a tiny pause he said on a note of curiosity, "Great muscles?''

Steve wasn't hugely muscular, but she had certainly noticed, when he stripped to the waist to help Zed dig out a rotted tree stump or re-lay a path, that his shoulders and arms had a nicely developed masculine outline.

"Anyway," she said hurriedly, "we have one firm promise—I told you about that, the violinist—and I have a few others to follow up—''

"Uh-huh." Then in the background Triss identified a female murmur, and Steve's voice became muffled as though he wasn't speaking into the phone or had covered it with his hand. "That's fine, hon, right there. Great." Then, more clearly he said, "That's good."

Triss had come to a dead stop. Something turned over unpleasantly in her stomach. Heat rose from her chest to her face. He wasn't alone on—in?—that hotel bed.

"Triss? You still there?"

"Yes," she said, almost choking. "Um…I can't really tell you any more."

"Well," he said, "I haven't been flexing any muscles—'' the amusement hadn't faded ''—but I've been talking about Kurakaha over here, and a couple of people are quite interested.''

"What sort of people?" Triss asked cautiously, trying to banish the picture in her mind of some woman beside him, touching him, unbuttoning his shirt—if he was wearing one at all—kissing that broad chest…

"Film people," he said. "It would be something new for Kurakaha, a module on filmmaking."

Magnus had always been scathing about what he

called a bastard craft. "I...don't know about that."
She was distracted, anxious now to get off the phone.
"I have to go. Someone's waiting for me," she lied.

"I'll do some more groundwork, and we'll talk it
over when I get back."

"Yes. Goodbye."

She put down the receiver before he had a chance
to say more. Her hands were trembling, and her face
was still hot.

Steve was an adult. What he did, who he slept with,
was nothing to do with her. Only it was bad taste to
mix his very private pleasure with a business call. That
was what had upset her—anyone would have been embarrassed. It was no big deal.

Yet, for the rest of the day she couldn't quite banish
the sick feeling in her stomach.

When Steve returned, Triss and Hana were preparing
the evening meal. He came in with a cabin bag slung
over his shoulder and a larger bag swinging from one
hand.

Hana, rinsing a cabbage at the sink, turned to him
with a big smile, shaking water from her hands to go
and give him a warm kiss on the cheek. "Hi there,
nice to see you back, Steve!"

"Thanks, Hana." His eyes went past her to find
Triss standing at the counter, peeling purple-skinned
kumara and dropping the golden-fleshed sweet potatoes into a pot. "Triss." He walked over and touched
his lips to her cool skin. "Hi."

She tried to smile but her shoulders were stiff and
the curve of her lips was unconvincing. "Hello," she
said woodenly.

Steve's eyes searched her face. "Everything okay?"

"Yes," Triss managed. "Of course."

He nodded, studying her before turning away. "I'll go and unpack. Be with you later."

Over dinner she felt him watching her, even though they were seated at separate tables. Afterward he approached her and said, "When can we talk?"

"Aren't you jet-lagged?"

"Not particularly."

"I've kept you up to date on everything that's been happening while you were away."

"You've been very good at it. But I have things to tell you."

Triss shrugged. "In half an hour then, my office?"

"I was thinking of somewhere a bit less formal."

She bit her lip. "All right. Come up to the flat if you like."

He arrived with a bottle of red wine in his hand. "Duty-free," he said. "I thought we might crack it open."

"To celebrate your return?" Triss asked, leading him into the small sitting room. She didn't feel like celebrating, but maybe it would help to loosen the tight feeling in her chest that had succeeded the first dismaying flood of pleasure she'd felt when he'd walked in this afternoon.

"If you find me a corkscrew I'll open it."

He followed her to the kitchenette, where she reached into a cupboard, becoming self-conscious when her short cotton top rode above the waistband of her jeans.

Quickly she turned with the corkscrew in her hand.

The look in his eyes made her breathless, then he took the corkscrew from her and turned away to put the bottle on the counter and remove the cork.

Trying to steady her lurching heart, Triss found two glasses and Steve poured the wine, handed one to her and raised his, touching them together. "Cheers."

"Cheers," she echoed before taking a sip of the rich, smooth liquid.

Back in the sitting room, she indicated the small sofa while she seated herself on one of the matching chairs.

Steve drank some of his wine. "I have a musical director who's willing to conduct a film module. Very experienced, works for major studios and conducts courses around America."

"You know Magnus wouldn't have—"

Steve leaned forward. "Even Magnus was willing to try new, experimental things in the short courses. Okay, so he had blind spot about film, I know. But these kids deserve the chance to find out about one of the most vital—and potentially lucrative—fields for their talent."

"A return air fare from the States is expensive."

"I'll pay the fare."

Triss chewed briefly on her lip, but could think of no other argument. And he was right—Magnus had been peculiarly prejudiced about that one field of artistic endeavor. "All right," she agreed, quelling a niggle of guilt. "We'll try it." She had no doubt the students would leap at it.

They discussed other plans for the following year, and after an hour or so Triss was surprised to see how much the level of the wine bottle had dropped. Steve reached over and doled out the remaining two inches between them.

"Is that all the business?" he asked, relaxing against the sofa.

"For now." Triss sipped more wine, feeling quite pleasantly mellow.

They sat in silence for a while, and she slipped deeper into the comfortable haze. A yawn made her cover her mouth, and Steve smiled at her. "Been burning the candle?"

Triss shook her head. "Only working."

"Not good for you," he said. "All work and no play."

About to retort that it wasn't good for him either, she recalled the woman's voice in the background of his phone call, the lazy approval in his as he'd spoken to her.

"What is it?" He must have noticed a change in her expression.

"Nothing. I was just…thinking."

He raised his brows interrogatively but didn't press the point when she failed to elaborate. After a while he said, "How have you been?"

"Me? I'm fine."

"Still lonely?"

She had more or less admitted on the beach with him that she needed company. "I'll get over it."

His brief look was piercing before he went back to gently swirling the remains of his wine. "I miss him, too," he said in a low voice. "Even though I hadn't seen him in years, it's different now." Quickly he finished his drink, but sat nursing his empty glass. "A man like that leaves a big hole."

Triss smiled a sad agreement. Steve got up, putting his glass down on the table between them. Triss stood, too, moving toward the door to see him out. But as she reached his side her bare arm brushed against his sleeve. He turned his head and somehow they were face-to-face, his fingers curled firmly about her arm, his eyes gravely looking into her widened stare.

For a breathless, timeless moment they were like two statues—or two parts of one statue—less than a hand span apart, his questioning eyes seeking answers in her dazed ones.

When he began to bend his head toward her, his gaze on her mouth, she knew she should step back, break his hold, stop what was about to happen. But she didn't.

The first tentative touch of his lips brought a warm shock, and her mouth trembled, then parted as his kiss firmed and sought her reciprocation. She was consumed by a reckless curiosity, wanting to know the taste and texture of his mouth, knowing he was enjoying hers. His hand moved up her arm, his other hand now on her waist, drawing her closer so their bodies touched, fitted together, hers conforming to his, her back a taut curved bow against the tensile strength of his supporting arm.

The kiss was a blend of passion and constraint, a tender exploration, and when he drew his mouth from hers at last and looked into her eyes, he looked almost as stunned as she felt.

Triss blinked and her spine straightened. She gasped, pulling away from his slackened hold.

She heard him mutter a swear word, and then he turned his back, striding toward the door. He hauled it

open and the next instant he was gone, leaving her
staring at the wooden panels as he closed it behind him
with a snap of finality.

Triss stood with a hand over her throbbing lips. She
could still taste him, feel the imprint of his mouth.

In the morning she had a long, cool shower, desperate to dispel ragged memories of erotic dreams. But
try as she would to persuade herself that the kiss had
been part of the dreams, she knew it had been real.

Her husband was scarcely in his grave, and she'd
been kissing another man—kissing Steve of all people!

And for a few minutes that cold, empty space inside
her had been filled by the feel of his body, the taste of
his mouth, the gentle strength of his arms about her.
She'd felt safe and warm and...loved.

An illusion, born out of loneliness and fueled by
alcohol. Steve didn't love her—he was only now beginning to show some semblance of trust in her, after
apparently hating her for years. And she couldn't be
falling for anyone so soon after losing Magnus.

She was late for breakfast, after debating whether to
go down for it at all and deciding not to take the cow-
ard's way out. In any case it would only delay the
inevitable. She couldn't avoid Steve forever.

His table was full and he scarcely glanced at her,
but when she sat down she still felt the impact of that
quick, keen scrutiny. He hadn't forgotten last night any
more than she had.

Later he came into her office, after a light tap on the
door. She knew who it was without looking up from
the mail she was opening, and knew that he'd approached the desk while she took a second to make

sure her face would give nothing away of the chaos of her emotions.

"Are you okay?" he asked her quietly.

"Of course." She put down the sheet of paper in her hand in case it shook and gave her away. "Maybe I should have a hangover but actually I'm fine." She was aware that her voice sounded a shade brittle, but was pleased that it was quite even.

"You weren't drunk."

"The wine impaired my judgment."

Steve was silent for long enough that she was compelled to look up. He was staring at her with hard speculation. "Excuses, Triss."

Damn him, why didn't he just let the matter lie? "There's no need to discuss this," she said flatly, looking away from him to ostensibly study the letter before her. They would just have to put the incident behind them, try to forget it had ever happened.

But Steve had different ideas. He said, "Maybe you're right about that," and then he leaned across the desk, placed a hand under her chin and kissed her.

This time there was no warning. Her lips parted in astonishment, and there was a studied provocation in the way he forced them farther open.

It lasted only a second, then he released her and stepped back, shoving both his hands into the pockets of his casual trousers, while Triss shot to her feet, the typing chair scooting back.

She had to lean her hands on the desktop to steady herself. "What do you think you're doing?"

"Just testing." His eyes glittered.

"Well, go and conduct your experiments on someone else!"

He was looking at her exactly as she imagined a naturalist might look at a new species of bug. "Who are you angry with?" he asked. "Yourself or me?"

Both, she might have told him, if she'd been willing to discuss this at all. She was guilty and embarrassed and horrified at herself. And surely he should be feeling the same? "I'm busy," she said, sitting down again and drawing a letter toward her, "and I'm sure you have things to do."

She didn't look up until he had left, snapping the door shut behind him. Then she put down the letter, which she couldn't read anyway because the print was dancing in front of her eyes, and let out a pent-up breath.

She managed to avoid being alone with Steve for several days, although she was aware of him watching her, often with a strangely baffled expression.

Grant McKay brought over some free firewood cut on his property, and while Zed and Steve were helping him stack it in the woodshed where it would dry out before winter, Triss went out to thank him and invite him to have a cup of tea before he left.

The four of them sat around one of the dining tables, the men hoeing into some of Hana's baking. Grant was especially appreciative, and Triss said, "You must take some cake home. I'll wrap it for you." It was a small return for the wood.

After he had gone Zed returned outside but Steve helped Triss to clear up. "Is Grant on his own?" he asked as he carried the cups to the dishwasher.

"Yes. His wife had left him before he bought the

farm here.'' Triss carefully replaced a few biscuits in a container. "I guess he wanted to make a new start."

Steve placed the cups in the machine and closed it. "No children?"

"Two. They spend time with him but live with their mother. He'd like to have them more often, only it's difficult with the farm to look after. They're too young to be left unsupervised and their mother doesn't like him taking them with him when he's working." Triss placed the container on a shelf.

"Why hasn't he married again?"

Triss turned to see him standing a few feet away, looking at her with disconcertingly penetrating eyes. "I don't know. He could be afraid of another failed marriage, or he just hasn't found anyone to love."

He hadn't taken his gaze from her. He seemed to be trying to penetrate her skull. "Like you loved Magnus?"

Chapter Eight

Triss swallowed. "Yes," she said huskily, her eyes defiant.

It might not have been the consuming passion that poets and songwriters celebrated, but in its own terms it had been real all the same.

Steve's eyes flickered. She could see the hard doubt in his face.

He didn't believe her, and she had undoubtedly re-inforced his opinion by returning his kiss the other night. Had that too been an experiment—just testing? Her skin crawled with humiliation.

"You don't understand," she told him. "You never did."

"So tell me." His voice was curiously intense.

Triss shook her head. "No." She wasn't about to hold up her marriage to his lynx-eyed inspection.

To her surprise he looked slightly discomfited then. He might even have been going to apologize, but

Hana entered the kitchen with her children at her heels, and the moment passed.

Later that week, while Triss was pulling weeds from the vegetable patch, Grant called in again.

"I thought that was Zed's job," he said.

Triss stood up, pulling off her gardening gloves. "It gets me out in the fresh air," she explained. "What can I do for you, Grant?"

"Nothing. I left a side of mutton in the kitchen with Hana. Just…ah…thought I'd say hello while I'm here."

Triss smiled at him. "Thank you."

Grant cleared his throat. "I was wondering…if you'd like to come with me to the Farming Association's fund-raising dinner-dance next Saturday night. I er don't have a partner and…well, I thought it'd be nice."

After a moment of blankness, she said, "Did Hana put you up to this?" Lately Hana had been hinting it was time she had some social life.

"Hell no!" Grant said. "Only, Magnus has been gone a while now, and I know how it is when…you know…you're on your own. I thought you might not mind…"

"Of course I don't mind! It's kind of you to ask." And, giving herself no chance to think about it, she added, "I'd like to."

"Great!" His smile widened. "I'll pick you up about six-thirty, okay?"

Triss nodded. "Okay."

Grant understood loss and grief. She knew he'd taken the breakup of his marriage hard, and after Magnus's death he'd been a true friend although not a specially close one.

She watched him walk away, a jauntiness to his step she'd never noticed before. He paused and waved to her before disappearing round the house. Smiling, she waved back, and when he'd gone she returned to the little heap of weeds she'd pulled, and saw Steve standing not far away, his eyes fixed on her face.

He strolled toward her. "You look happy."

Happy? An exaggeration, surely. Triss shrugged. "It's not a crime."

"I wasn't suggesting it is. What did Grant want?"

"He brought us some meat."

"Nice of him."

"He's a very nice man."

Steve looked at her sharply.

Triss drew in a breath and met his eyes. "He asked me to go to the Farming Association dance with him."

His eyes narrowing, Steve said, "And you accepted."

"Yes." Triss moistened her lips. "It's months since—"

"I know how long it is since Magnus died."

"Then…"

"What do you want me to say, Triss? That I give you permission?"

"Of course not! I don't need your permission or anyone else's."

"True," Steve said. "I hope you enjoy yourself."

He wheeled then and walked rapidly away as if he didn't trust himself near her anymore, leaving her unsettled and feeling prickly and defensive. She donned her gloves again and pulled a few more weeds, her mind skittering this way and that. She *would* damn well enjoy herself, she decided, obscurely angry.

The thick, tough stem she was hauling on broke away in her hand. The wretched weed would have to be dug out. Crossly she picked up a gardening fork and plunged it into the recalcitrant earth, working it back and forth. The root was deep and stubborn and by the time she hauled it triumphantly from its bed she was panting.

But she'd won, got rid of the thing, just as one day she'd get rid of the memory of Steve's kiss that seemed to have taken permanent root in her mind. Maybe going out with Grant would help.

She dressed with care in a pretty frock with a flared skirt and a bare neckline. Grant told her she looked wonderful and seemed to mean it. He looked scrubbed and groomed himself, and slightly anxious. Triss set out to put him at his ease.

The food was good, the entertainment fun, and Grant was a competent if not inspired dancer. Triss was rusty herself but she enjoyed the music and she liked the protective feeling of Grant's arms when he folded them about her to dance.

It was well after midnight when he delivered her to the back door of the house and accompanied her up the steps.

Stifling a yawn, she asked, "Would you like a cup of coffee? Or tea?"

He hesitated, shook his head. "You're tired."

Triss didn't argue. "Thank you, Grant. I had a good time."

"Me, too." His hand touched her arm and lingered. "Maybe we can do something like this again."

"Maybe," she agreed. There seemed no reason not to.

"Good night, Triss."

She knew he was going to kiss her, and didn't resist. It would be a nice way to end his evening, and somewhere in the back of her mind was a question that she wanted answered.

His lips were cool and tentative, but when she let hers part slightly under their pressure he became more confident and slid his arm about her waist.

It was pleasant and not too passionate, entirely suitable for a first kiss after a first date. She'd liked it, Triss told herself as they drew apart.

But, she had to admit when she'd let herself into the house and the sound of Grant's car was fading outside, her reaction had been nothing like the storm of wanton sensation she'd experienced when Steve kissed her.

She had almost persuaded herself that her feelings then had been simply a natural reflex after being celibate for too long, very little to do with the man who had evoked it. She might have felt the same about any reasonably attractive male who took her in his arms. Especially after drinking nearly half a bottle of wine.

She'd had wine tonight, too. Grant was just as handsome, just as strong as Steve, and she liked him. They liked each other. Whatever shifts had come about in her uncomfortable relationship with Steve, liking had hardly entered the equation.

A few days later Triss tactfully refused another invitation from Grant, saying she wasn't ready yet to start dating on a regular basis.

Perhaps hoping to change her mind, he was around often in the next few weeks, usually with the excuse of a gift of food for the House. And once to help Zed and Steve and some of the boys fell a huge old totara that had rotted at the base and was threatening to come down on the roof with the next high wind. Afterward Hana gave the three men beer in the kitchen, where Triss found them standing about, leaning on the nearest counter or table and discussing the latest rugby series.

Grant straightened and switched his attention to her, his blue eyes eagerly fastened on her face while they made small talk. Behind his shoulder she could see Steve watching them, a beer can in his hand, his expression cynically amused.

When Grant had left, Steve was still there, nursing the can. His eyes swept her from head to toe, he lifted the can to his lips and drained it, then gave her an enigmatic look and tossed the can into the recycling container under the worktable. "What are you going to do about him?" he asked softly.

Zed had clumped out after Grant, and Hana was rattling cutlery in the dining room.

"Do?" Triss echoed.

"Was he as obvious when Magnus was alive?"

"Don't be disgusting! Grant is a good friend and neighbor. He always was."

"Oh, yeah." Steve's mouth twisted. "Well, he'd sure like to be more than that now."

It was probably true but although she liked Grant, Triss wasn't going to encourage him to think it was going to happen. She was trying to be normally friendly without getting his hopes up, and it was difficult enough without Steve sniping from the sidelines. "He told you that, did he?" she inquired, knowing full well that Steve was guessing.

"Didn't need to," Steve replied laconically. "His

tongue practically drags on the floor every time you come in sight.''

''Must you be so crude?'' she flashed. ''Maybe you should put your own tongue back where it belongs, and keep your eyes to yourself while you're about it!''

She hadn't meant to say that, it had spilled from her subconscious, a gut knowledge that she'd suppressed until this moment, but she couldn't help a spurt of satisfaction when she saw his eyes darken and a hint of color appear in his cheeks, even as his mouth went hard.

Bull's-eye, she thought triumphantly, and marched from the room before he could retaliate.

The next day she had to seek Steve out to get a check signed. She tapped on the door of the music room where he was working, and cautiously opened it.

He sat at the electronic keyboard with his back to her, a pad and pencil on top of the instrument while his hands riffled over the keys.

''I'm sorry to disturb you,'' she said.

''No problem. What did you want?''

She gave him the check and he signed his name beside hers just as Zed appeared in the doorway. ''Triss? Hana said you had another letter you want to send.''

Hastily she inserted the check into the already stamped and addressed envelope and handed it to him.

When Zed had gone she made to leave, too, but Steve caught her wrist in a light clasp. ''Wait.''

''Why?'' She looked down at his hand, then warily at his face.

''Because I don't want you to go.''

Triss lifted her brows interrogatively but he only stared at her as if trying to fathom something out.

Then abruptly he said, "I guess I deserved that slam you delivered before you left yesterday."

"I'm not…involved with Grant," she said.

"Didn't you enjoy your date?"

She blinked, pulling her hand away. "I had a very enjoyable evening."

"Did he kiss you good-night?"

Triss stiffened. "You can't expect me to answer that!"

Steve gave a short laugh. "He did, then. I guess you enjoyed that, too."

"As a matter of fact, yes!"

He said after a moment, "As much as you enjoyed kissing me?"

"I'm not comparing!" A lie, her conscience jeered.

She made rapidly for the half-open door, but he moved swiftly and slammed it shut in her face, barring her exit.

"I've never been able to fathom you, Triss," he said. "You kissed *me* as if your life depended on it, then the next day you didn't want to know."

"I'd been drinking that night, and I was…confused. It could have been anyone."

"You'd have kissed any man who happened to be about?"

Of course she wouldn't have. But he wasn't any man, he was Steve, and their relationship was complicated enough as it was. She didn't want it spiraling out of control, causing problems for the House. "I won't discuss this anymore."

"All right," he said grimly. "If you don't want to talk…"

He reached for her and she tried to step back, too late. His powerful arms imprisoned her and his mouth assaulted hers, smothering her protest. Her hands, jammed against the warm cage of his chest, uselessly pushed at him. She was acutely conscious of every inch of that hard masculine body against hers, and when she lifted a foot and kicked at his ankle he swung her off her feet, turning her until the door was at her back, thrusting his thigh between hers.

Triss gasped, and he took lightning advantage, parting her lips farther, the kiss becoming persuasive, perilously erotic.

Her heartbeat was thunderous, and a dangerous, fierce elation coursed through her. Every nerve a river of flame, she was drowning in sensation, her resistance consumed by the white-hot heat of desire. She curled her fists against his shirt, willing herself to be strong.

Only pride—and anger—kept her from completely melting, throwing her arms about his neck and begging for more. It took a huge amount of willpower to keep her body rigid and ungiving, even as her mouth involuntarily softened under the coaxing movements of his. But she wouldn't kiss him back.

At last his mouth drew away, inches from hers, and with his hand spanning her throat he looked down at her with brilliant, fathomless eyes, his face taut and unsmiling. "I suppose I should apologize," he said. "Again."

Triss, her eyes held by his, swallowed painfully. "Yes."

"But I'm not sorry."

She was mesmerized, unable to look away from the glittering gaze that held hers with a strange mixture of desire and anger.

He said, "I want to do it again." His thumb grazed her moistened lower lip, and she trembled, unable to stop herself.

The glitter in his eyes intensified. "I want to touch you," he said, his voice very low. His hand slipped down her neck, one finger lingering briefly in the hollow at its base, then the lapels of her blouse parted, a button slipped open and his palm cupped her breast.

Triss couldn't take her eyes from his, even as a throaty gasp escaped her. She ought to be fighting him, pushing him away. Some delicious paralysis seemed to have taken hold of her.

His thumb moved across her skin above her bra. He watched the hot color flood her cheeks and her teeth sink into her lower lip. His smile was tight and triumphant. He pressed his thigh against her and she shuddered.

"Steve…"

His thumb was inside her bra now, finding the furled bud that reacted instantly to his teasing touch. He hooked his fingers under the strap and eased it down, freeing the firm globe of her breast. "Triss?"

Triss drew a sharp breath. Her eyelids fluttered down. "I…we shouldn't do this."

"Why not?" His voice was low, close to her ear. His fingers moved on her, insidiously. "Do want to stop?"

She should say yes. She had to say it. Her lips wouldn't form the word.

"Tell me to stop," he said, his mouth against the tender hollow below her ear, "and I will." He kissed her jawline, dragging his lips to her mouth, his breath warm.

Her lips parted but no sound came. He waited for a

long second, then claimed them with his. And this time she couldn't pretend. Her mouth opened for him, clung, invited, welcomed, and she arched her back slightly as his palm cradled her breast, wanting him to feel its softness and hardness. His hand was roughened from working in the garden, and the delicious friction brought a small sound of pleasure from her that he answered with a guttural groan.

It was Steve who finally broke the kiss, reluctantly lifting his mouth, looking into her slowly opening eyes with a glazed dark stare. His hand still caressing her, he said in a low voice, "Let me come to you tonight."

Emerging sluggishly from the trance of passion, Triss shivered, blinked. She didn't want to think, but he was waiting for an answer.

"Or will you come to me?" he said, urgently.

Although her whole body was screaming, *Yes, yes!* somewhere deep in her mind a distant voice of caution and sanity clamored to be heard.

"Triss?" His mouth found hers again, questioning, brief. His hand stilled as he raised his head.

Her teeth bit down on her lower lip, the small hurt helping to clear her mind. Unable to speak, she shook her head.

A frown appeared between his brows. "Triss!" His mouth came down again on hers—hard, desperate.

She jerked her head away. "No!"

Steve took his hand from her breast at last to grasp her chin and turn her face upward to his accusing gaze. *"No?"* He looked incredulous.

Feebly she pushed against him. "Let me go."

His eyes were momentarily murderous, then he dropped his hands from her and stepped back, staring at her.

Triss fished inside her blouse, readjusting her strap, and then with trembling fingers did up the buttons—three of them were undone now, and she'd been totally unaware.

Steve hadn't taken his eyes off her. "You are unbelievable," he muttered.

Rallying her forces, such as they were, Triss tilted her chin. "Because I don't want to sleep with you?" she challenged him, trying to sound scornful. But her breathing was uneven and her voice wobbled.

He gave a wolfish grin. "You do *want,*" he asserted. "So what sort of game are you playing now?"

"It isn't a game! I don't w—" She stopped for a steadying breath. "I don't intend to sleep with you—not tonight, not ever. This can't happen again."

"Can't?"

Vehemently Triss shook her head. "Won't. I won't let it."

His tone deadly soft, he said, "Would you like to take a bet on that?"

A trickle of forbidden sensation ran down her spine. *"Don't!"* she cried, on a note almost of anguished panic.

"Did you do this to Grant?" he asked her.

"Do what?"

"Get him worked up and leave him dangling. Is that how you operate? I guess that's what you did with that poor student you were fooling about with before I left—and how many more since?" Ignoring her astonished gasp, he went on. "I thought you'd changed since I left—matured, maybe worked out whatever it was that drove you. But I guess not. Is it a power thing? The boys must be easy game, but I'm no boy anymore. And I don't play nice—"

"What?" Her brain reeling, Triss finally found her voice, cutting him off. "What are you *talking* about?"

This was insane!

"You know what I'm talking about," Steve said. "What was his name? Mark—Mark Powell. Remember him? Of course I don't know how many others there've been since…"

Mark Powell. Triss did remember him. She had made a bad mistake, one she'd taken care never to repeat. "You don't know what you're saying," she whispered, feeling sick. All along—for years—Steve had believed…what? That she was some kind of siren, seducing the young men her husband was trying to help? "You saw us," she said. One incident and he'd built a case, held it against her all this time.

"You're not denying it, then." His voice was flat. He gave a small, harsh laugh. "Yes, I saw you kissing."

"Were you hiding behind the trees?"

"I didn't need to hide. The two of you were too… occupied to notice anyone approaching the grotto. A pity it wasn't Magnus. He might have believed the evidence of his own eyes."

Triss's cheeks went cold. *"You told Magnus?"*

His mouth was grim. "Not for quite a while. It goes against the grain to tell tales, but in the end I figured it was too important to the school to let the matter lie." Seeing her stricken face, he said bitterly, "You had no need to worry. He didn't believe me."

"He never even asked me about it!" Magnus had trusted her, given no credence to the story. Belated gratitude warmed her heart.

"You had him thoroughly twisted about your little finger," Steve said bitterly. "He told me I must have been mistaken. Nothing would convince him you might not have been pure as driven snow.''

Horrified and sickened, she demanded, ''Why didn't you tell *me* you'd seen us? Why not ask me about it yourself?''

''You could hardly explain that away.''

''You didn't give me the chance! Because you wanted to believe the worst of me—you wanted Magnus to get rid of me.''

Contemptuously he said, ''Now why would I want that?''

''You resented me. I understood that, but I hoped we could become friends.''

''Friends!''

Nonplussed, Triss said, ''I know it was difficult for you, but surely you were old enough to accept me as Magnus's wife.''

''I accepted that! I was twenty-three and not stupid. What I couldn't accept was you coming on to me.''

Chapter Nine

"C-coming on...?" The world spun. Triss shook her head to clear her whirling thoughts. "I don't believe I'm hearing this."

"Are you denying that, too?"

"*Of course* I'm denying it!" Pure rage flooded through her. "You can't accuse me of that!" Although he just had. "What did I ever do to make you imagine I was...was interested in you in that way?"

He made a scornful sound. "Have you forgotten? You followed me—"

"*Followed* you?" The man must have been paranoid—delusional. Beyond ridiculous, this was bizarre.

"How else did you manage to turn up when I was alone in the garden or in a music room?"

That was the construction he'd put on her useless attempts to find some point of communication? That she'd wanted some kind of sexual response from him?

He said, "So you don't remember the night you tracked me down in one of the music rooms?"

Triss remembered, all right. Magnus had found some of Steve's music among his own papers and asked her to find him and return it because Steve might be wondering where he'd left it.

For weeks she'd been trying to establish some kind of harmonious relationship with Magnus's difficult protégé. Their initial meeting had been less than promising. Triss had been caught off guard because although Magnus had mentioned the "boy" he'd semi-adopted, who shared his apartment, he'd failed to tell her Steve's age. Imagining a youth of about sixteen, she'd been instead confronted with a man as old as herself. A man whose face seemed to close down at his first sight of her, who extended his hand only reluctantly when she offered hers, and whose incredulous glance at his foster parent had clearly questioned Magnus's judgment, if not his sanity.

Recovering from her surprise, she'd given him her warmest smile and said something inanely conventional about looking forward to getting to know him. He hadn't returned the sentiment, and in the ensuing weeks he'd rebuffed her every time she tried.

He'd moved out of the second bedroom into a single room in the main house, against Magnus's objection that there was no need. Triss too urged him to stay, striving to infuse sincerity into her voice, but he'd merely given her an enigmatic, contained smile and a strange, cool glance, and continued to pack his few belongings into cardboard boxes.

Deep down she'd been relieved, even grateful. While Magnus could see no problem, Triss knew she'd find it easier to settle into her new life if she could count on sometimes being truly alone with her husband.

But when she sought out Steve to quietly thank him
for his consideration and assure him he was welcome
to visit whenever he wanted, he said, "I didn't do it
for you. I need my own space."

He'd been busy tying tomato plants to stakes in the
garden, and she'd stepped forward to help, holding the
plants for him while she tried to continue the conversation and establish some common ground, but Steve
had been markedly uncooperative, and after a few
minutes of being answered in polite monosyllables
she'd given up. When the job was finished he'd muttered a curt word of thanks that made it obvious he
was dismissing her. Defeated, she'd left.

The younger boys had accepted her remarkably
quickly. Some were shy but others were eager to talk,
curious about her and how she'd come to marry Magnus. A few told her candidly they'd thought he was
gay. Triss laughed at them and didn't elaborate.

"The boys like you," Magnus said to her, with mild
surprise and pleased approval.

But her people skills had failed her as far as Steve
was concerned. He seemed determined to hold himself
aloof, and for Magnus's sake that disturbed her. Not a
man who easily revealed his feelings, Magnus had
shown no signs of noticing the strained atmosphere
between his wife and Steve, but he couldn't be completely unaware.

Every overture she made met with the same stone
wall of indifference. The night she delivered the music
score, he'd tossed it on the piano in the small practice
room and stood waiting for her to leave, but in the
doorway she paused, pushed the door almost closed to
discourage interruptions and turned to Steve, determined on yet another effort to get through to him.

He looked surprised and suspicious, guardedly folding his arms.

Unaccountably rattled, Triss gave him a nervous smile. "I...I think we need to talk."

Without moving he said, "So...talk."

She tried another smile. "I'm not sure how to start."

Steve gave her no help. He seemed as immovable as a rock.

Triss spread her hands in a helpless little gesture. "Steve—I don't want to come between you and Magnus."

"You haven't."

The blunt contradiction stymied her. "I hope you're right. But I feel I've pushed you out of your home."

"It wasn't mine."

"Not legally maybe, but—"

"I'm not a child," Steve said. "And Magnus isn't my father."

"I know." She cast around for something more to say. "You were a bit of a surprise," she told him lightly. "I'd kind of assumed you were still in your teens." She moistened her lips. "I did hope we'd be friends."

"Friends." He seemed to be trying out the word, as if the possibility had never occurred to him. He looked past her, his eyes taking on a glazed expression.

"Steve?" Puzzled, she went to him and lightly laid a hand on his arm. He was wearing a short-sleeved T-shirt, and the fuzz of hair on his skin tickled her fingers, while her eyes and her lowered voice pleaded with him. "I'd really like us to be closer, Steve. It can't be that difficult for us to get along. In the end, don't we both want the same thing?"

Surely he didn't want Magnus hurt, any more than

she did. They needed to build some kind of rapport for the sake of the man they both loved. "Magnus may turn a blind eye for a wh—"

His hand closed about her wrist in a bone-breaking grip. The remainder of her speech—that sooner or later Magnus would recognize Steve's determined refusal to relate to her and be distressed by it—was lost in a gasp of pain as he removed her hand from his arm and flung it away from him.

He was glaring at her with a kind of stunned fury that bewildered her. Hands clenched at his sides, he took a step forward, and instinctively she fell back, fear tautening the skin of her face. He looked ready to do her some physical injury. Only because she'd touched him? She gazed at him warily, anticipating his next move, ready to duck, or counteract it.

Then he strode past her and found the door handle, throwing the door open as he stepped aside. "Get out," he said.

"I don't underst—"

"Get…out." He spoke between clenched teeth.

Frightened and confused, she stumbled past him and heard the door slam behind her. She paused for only an instant, then fled along the corridor and up the stairs to her and Magnus's quarters.

What was wrong with the man? He must have some kind of problem—perhaps not surprisingly after what she knew had been a checkered childhood. But she'd never seen him like that before.

"Did Steve ever have counseling?" she demanded of Magnus, who was working on some papers in the living room.

Magnus glanced up over the half spectacles he wore

for reading. "Before he came here. He was pretty scathing about it. Why do you ask?"

"Because he…"

He…what? Her wrist still throbbed, but she knew his intention hadn't been to hurt her, only to get rid of the fingers she'd laid so lightly, tentatively, on his arm. An extreme reaction, but hardly an attack. Did he have an aversion to being touched? She recalled his tardy response to her proffered handshake when they met.

But she'd seen him in contact sports with the boys, grinning as he accepted their arms about his shoulders after scoring, their pats and mock punches of congratulation.

It was her touch he couldn't stand. Or perhaps any female touch at all. "Has he ever had girlfriends?"

"A few. Well, quite likely more than I'd know about. He doesn't confide. They certainly like him—girls." Magnus looked at her curiously. "Are you all right? You look flushed."

"I ran up the stairs." The excuse was automatic.

Magnus smiled. "Couldn't wait to get back to me, eh?"

Comforted by the familiarity of his gentle teasing, Triss smiled back. "Of course." She walked to his side and dropped a kiss on his forehead, then leaned against the desk. "Did you miss me?"

He patted her knee. "Always." Taking off his glasses, he began polishing them with the edge of his jacket. "Don't worry about Steve, my dear. He learned early to withhold his emotions and reserve judgment. He'll come round in time."

So Magnus had noticed. As she'd said, he was turning a blind eye. And Steve, he was warning her, didn't like to be rushed. Perhaps she'd tried too hard to penetrate the barriers he'd erected against her.

Instead she'd only aroused his anger. An anger so raw and elemental she'd cringed from it, and in succeeding weeks she'd tried her best to erase the incident from her mind.

Now the whole thing came flooding back in horrifying detail...because Steve had just accused her of coming on to him that night. And for the first time she saw the scene from his undoubtedly twisted point of view.

It explained why he'd been so furious. Why he'd flung off her casual, unthinking touch with such disgust. And even, perhaps, why he'd been so ready to conclude that she'd been inciting young Mark Powell to make love to her.

As if to confirm it, Steve said, "So, when I wouldn't play ball, you found someone more vulnerable to use your...skills on."

Triss tried to speak around a horrendous lump that blocked her throat. "You really believe this," she said finally. "Don't you?" Even now, when she'd thought he'd been coming round to actually liking her, as well as being unmistakably attracted sexually, he'd thought her capable of betraying Magnus in that way when he was alive. No wonder he'd not expected any scruples from her now her husband was dead.

"What else could I believe?"

"Maybe that Magnus wasn't stupid enough to marry the kind of slut you decided I was."

"Magnus didn't know much about women."

"He knew a hell of a lot more than you do! Actually Magnus had several relationships before he met me, only he kept them away from Kurakaha." She could see by the brief flicker of shock in his eyes that was news to him. But Magnus had been honest with her. "Tell me…'knowing' all this about me, how could you bring yourself to kiss me?"

He said slowly, "I figured you'd changed. Like I did when Magnus took me in hand. I'm in no position to throw stones."

"Gee, thanks!"

"I hadn't intended to dredge up past sins—"

"Oh, but you're having such fun! Don't stop now!"

"Do you think I enjoy this?"

"I think from the start you wanted to think the worst of me, for no reason except your own pathetic sense of insecurity—"

Steve gave a crack of startled laughter. "Where the hell does that idea come from?"

"It's not difficult to work out. You might have been legally adult when Magnus married me, but inside you were still a scared little boy, afraid of being rejected again. That's why you ran to Magnus instead of confronting me with your conclusions about what you thought you'd seen—"

"What I *had* seen. And as I said, I didn't want to tell Magnus. I stewed about it for weeks—"

"What you saw," Triss said ruthlessly, "was me and a frightened kid—"

"Mark was coming up twenty."

"Yes, too old to continue at the school, but immature and scared of what would happen to him when he left. His mother was an alcoholic, his father a bully who never gave her any money for the family on the grounds she'd spend it on drink, and Mark had younger brothers and sisters. He was torn between his music and looking after them. He'd been telling me all about it when he broke down in tears, and I gave him a hug.''

It had been her first mistake, though it would have taken a much harder heart than hers to ignore the deep sobs that Mark had tried unsuccessfully to stem.

She said, ''After he'd stopped crying I was holding him, waiting for him to be ready to move. When he lifted his face he looked so woebegone I gave him a kiss—on his cheek.''

Steve made a derisive sound.

''Then he…sort of lunged at me.''

Mark's lips, pressing feverishly on hers, had been hot and trembling, wet with salty tears, and her shock had mingled with wrenching pity. ''I pushed him away, but not violently. I didn't want—or need—to crush the poor kid completely. Well…he wasn't a kid physically, of course. I'd forgotten that, so what happened was partly my fault. After a few seconds he got the message. He kept on apologizing even though I told him I wasn't offended, only it mustn't happen again. He couldn't look me in the eye for days afterwards.''

She had no idea if Steve believed her or not. He regarded her with a brooding expression in his eyes, giving her no clue.

Helplessly she spread her hands. ''It was no big deal! And as for the night we talked in the practice room…all I was asking for was your friendship. It never occurred to me that you'd misconstrue everything I said.''

His mouth tightened. ''You said Magnus would turn a blind eye. If it didn't mean what I thought—''

''It meant that he'd been turning a blind eye to your

antagonism towards me! He was hoping we'd resolve it somehow.''

Steve gave no sign of even listening, let alone absorbing the words. His eyes were narrowed and suspicious, totally ungiving.

Her heart sinking, she said, ''Did you tell Magnus about that, too?''

''No.'' As if he felt compelled, he added, ''I couldn't.''

Thank God for small mercies. Triss's shoulders drooped in hopelessness. ''None of what you thought was true. But you'll believe what you want to—just as you did before.''

She wrenched open the door and he didn't stop her walking out.

Surely she should have felt better for telling him the facts. But she had the horrible feeling that he was totally unconvinced. She hurried down the corridor to her office, her fists clenched and her cheeks burning with temper.

So he'd thought she was reformed! That the love of a good man had brought about a change of heart—and morals. After nobly rejecting years ago what he'd thought were her advances, now he conceded she was worthy to share his bed.

It would be a cold day in hell before she did that.

Never had her bed seemed so lonely. For what must have been the hundredth time Triss turned over, adjusting her position yet again. Somewhere out in the night a morepork called its name. Distantly she heard the hum of traffic.

She kept hearing the echo of Steve's voice. *Will you come to me?* Her body throbbed, remembering his hand on her breast, the hard muscles of his thigh between hers.

Don't think about it.

Hand clenched on the pillow, she closed her eyes tightly, but all she could see was Steve's eyes resting on her, brilliant with desire, his thick black lashes lowering as he studied her mouth, just before he kissed her.

Opening her eyes wide until they hurt, she flung herself on her back, then shot upright as a sound penetrated the darkness. A sharp crack of wood from the stairs.

Her heart hammered, her ears straining for a repetition of the noise. She had assumed that after the quarrel they'd had, Steve wouldn't follow through on his intention to make love to her.

If he had come after all, did she have the strength to refuse him? Did she *want* to refuse him?

Another, fainter creak.

The old wood often made noises at night for no other reason than a change in temperature. No one was coming up the stairs. Certainly not Steve.

She waited for several minutes and nothing happened. But now she was wide awake. The window was open yet the room felt stuffy. There was no way she was going to be able to sleep.

Sighing, she got up and groped for the flat-heeled sandals she'd been wearing after dinner. Her cotton nightshirt was knee length and opaque, and she pulled a light, short-sleeved cardigan over it.

The stairs creaked again as she descended them slowly but confidently, not using the flashlight in her hand. Moonlight filtered through the long windows on the landing, and when she'd made it to the ground floor and let herself out, the landscape was washed in blue-white light.

The torch was only needed briefly on the darkest part of the path where the trees overhung it. She thought about walking along the road, but even in this quiet neck of the woods a woman in a nightgown walking alone at this time of night was probably inviting trouble. Instead she headed at a brisk pace for the knoll where the stone grotto stood. That way was mostly uphill and would make the best use of her surplus energy.

She was almost there, the torch switched off while she kept her eyes on the moonlit path ahead of her, when she glanced up at the summerhouse and thought she saw movement inside.

Pausing, she strained her eyes, but within the black shadow of the building saw nothing.

Imagination, she decided, or perhaps an inquisitive possum had forsaken the trees to explore. She'd better not startle it. Small and furry they might be, but possums had long claws and sharp teeth and might use them if they felt cornered.

Walking on, she kept her gaze on the doorway. The shadows shifted, a figure appeared, filling the stone arch, and Steve's voice said, ''Well, look who's here. Following me?''

Triss had nearly dropped the torch. She grasped it in slippery fingers and hauled breath into her lungs. ''Absolutely not!''

After a moment he said, ''You know, we really must stop meeting like this.''

''There's nothing I'd like more.''

After another short silence, Steve said, ''Why don't

you sit down?'' He moved aside to let her into the tiny space. His bare shoulders gleamed in the moonlight. He was wearing jeans with no shirt.

"No, thanks." She'd prefer to stay in the open this time. She contemplated simply turning and going back down the path, but didn't want to look as if she were running away.

Steve stood with his thumbs hooked into the waist of his jeans. "Couldn't sleep?"

Triss shook her head, not sure if he could see or not, not caring either. "Couldn't you?"

"I kept wondering if you'd turn up at my place, after all. But I quit that about an hour ago."

Earlier than she had. Triss found her lips were dry. She ran her tongue over them. "You surely didn't expect me to—after the things you said to me."

"Hope springs eternal," he said laconically. "And speaking of hope—was it true, what you told me? That I'd got it all wrong?"

"Every word." She couldn't help a tiny leap of hope of her own. "All of it."

For the longest time he didn't speak. Then he said, "You know that logically it seems unlikely."

Her heart plunged. She tried to examine the evidence the way he had, to look at it cold-bloodedly. But it was difficult not to be hurt. Hurt and angry. "I can't make you believe me," she said. "And I won't waste my time and breath trying."

"The odd thing is," he said, even as she made to turn away from him, "I do."

Triss felt as if she'd been hit in the solar plexus. "You...do?"

Slowly she turned again to face him. The moonlight

cast shadows, but she could see the jut of his brows and his eyes glinting below them.

"After I left for America," he said, "I kept thinking you'd be found out, that Magnus must realize soon he'd made a huge mistake. I expected you'd get sick of playing the doting wife or he'd come to his senses and throw you out. It didn't seem possible that you could have gone on fooling everyone but me. When it never happened, I figured you had some reason to hang on—like money."

Triss winced. "You were wrong! Utterly, absolutely wrong."

He shifted, his head bowed for a moment, as he seemed to contemplate the ground. "For what it's worth to you now...I'm sorry."

Triss drew a shaky breath. A huge weight had been lifted from her. "Thank you."

"Thank you? You should be throwing something at my head."

"Don't think I haven't been tempted, many times."

"I guess."

Seconds ticked by. Triss said, "I'm sorry about what happened between you and Magnus."

"Not your fault." He folded his arms and looked down again, pushing aside a few leaves on the path with his foot. "You were the catalyst, but we had philosophical differences. Sooner or later I'd have had to leave. He was holding me back."

"He was afraid you'd been seduced by the prospect of easy money."

Steve shook his head and laughed quietly. "It's good money, but it doesn't come easy. I put a lot of creative energy into my work. It's a different kind of creativity, granted. One that Magnus couldn't for some reason appreciate. The idea of art for art's sake is fine and pure, only it doesn't pay the bills. That's important to me.''

''Paying the bills?''

''Making my own way, earning a living without handouts or string pulling from anyone, taking responsibility for my debts. That's why I stuck around tutoring here after getting my degree—and why I'm back.''

''You've more than repaid your debt to Magnus,'' she told him. ''He shouldn't have left his will like that. It was unfair, forcing you to leave what you'd built. You don't owe him anymore.''

He shrugged, looking up into the blackness of the trees. ''That's one debt I can never repay sufficiently.''

Triss took a deep breath. ''The will didn't actually say you have to live at Kurakaha.'' And now he knew he could trust her, what was there to keep him here? She swallowed on an aching lump that had lodged in her throat.

''Do you want me to go?''

''No.'' The very thought brought a sharp desolation.

Maybe he was waiting for her to elaborate, but she could think of nothing more to add.

Quietly he said, ''Thank you.''

A night breeze rustled through the trees, and something whirred by Triss's cheek, then caught in her hair. Her stifled shriek brought Steve to her side, even as she tried to shake the intruder away.

''Don't move,'' he ordered, catching her arm. ''You'll only tangle it further.''

''Is it a huhu?'' she asked, with spurious calm. The huge flying beetles were harmless, she reminded herself, but her skin crawled with panic all the same.

"It's a puriri moth," Steve answered, his fingers in her hair. "Hold still while I get it out. There."

The green moth was almost as big as his palm, its wings fluttering feebly as it struggled upright. Then it waved them more strongly and rose into the air, disappearing among the trees.

"All right?" Steve's hand smoothed her mussed hair.

"I wasn't really scared," she lied. "It startled me."

"Sure." His voice was soothing, like his hand, which now rested at her nape. She realized how close he was, just before he exerted the slight pressure that brought their bodies in contact and lifted her face to him.

Chapter Ten

Triss didn't resist, knowing at some subconscious level that this had been inevitable from the moment she'd seen Steve emerge out of the grotto into the moonlight.

He kissed her forehead, and she felt the light, warm touch all the way to her toes. His lips closed her eyelids. Then his breath tickled her lips, and she parted them in invitation even before his mouth claimed hers in a kiss that was long and tender and sweet, full of unspoken promises.

She had her hands on his arms, and she slid them up to his bare shoulders, outlined the strong curves, found the taut planes of his neck and the tantalizing texture of his hair.

When he lifted his head her body was thrumming, ripples of anticipation running over her skin, and her breasts throbbed.

She saw the movement of his throat when he swallowed, and she smiled, then leaned forward to flick her tongue into the salty hollow at its base.

He said something inaudible but explosive, and his hands went to the buttons of her nightshirt. ''Tease!''

He parted the material that covered her breasts, allowing the slight cool breeze to lave them. For a moment he stood, just looking at her, then he touched her almost reverently, and she realized his hands were trembling.

''I've dreamed of this,'' he said, ''for months... years.''

When he hadn't even liked her? *Years?* But she didn't have time to think about that, because the surprising softness of his dark hair caressed her chin as he bent to brush his mouth across the swelling curves of her breasts, and she rocketed straight to another plane of sensation, all thought suspended.

She swayed. Only his arm clamped about her waist prevented her from falling. Her hands grasped his shoulders, raked into his hair, and she rose on tiptoe, gasping incoherent encouragement to his ministrations.

She ran her fingers through his hair again, tugging lightly to bring his mouth back to hers, open and eager for him. He didn't disappoint her, gentleness dispelled in the wanton ruthlessness of mutual desire. She locked her arms about his neck and lost all awareness of anything but the way he made her feel—and the way she knew she was making him feel.

Her heart was beating hard and fast. When he cupped his hand about her from behind she pressed closer, feeling his arousal snug to her body, and hot blood shot through her veins. Instinctively she moved against him.

He wrenched his mouth away, groaning deep in his

throat, and she heard his harsh breathing. "We can't finish this," he said. "Not properly—not here. I don't have anything with me."

Triss was almost beyond caring. She wanted nothing in the world but to strip him and herself and have him inside her, skin to skin, their naked bodies touching from head to toe. But common sense hadn't quite deserted her. "Do you want to stop now?"

He groaned again. "Stupid question!"

His arms tightened, both hands closing over her, and he lifted her to him, their mouths meeting again. She felt the pleasure, a tight knot that expanded and flowered and then centered, arrowing to the apex of her body before spreading again, flooding every part of her, so that she cried out against Steve's mouth on hers, wrapping her legs about him. Vaguely she heard him answer her with a guttural cry of his own, then he bucked against her, and was turning them, dizzyingly, everything whirling about her.

The moonlight filtering through her closed eyelids dimmed. Steve grasped her legs and she found smooth wood beneath her knees and she realized they were in the grotto, Steve on the wooden seat with his back to the wall while she straddled his lap.

His hand stroked her spine under the nightshirt, and his head rested against the stone behind him. His eyes were closed.

She kissed him, slow and sweet, and his lips answered her, even as his breathing gradually steadied.

Triss let her hand wander over his chest again, not with passion this time but with a sort of quiet, tender wonder.

She stirred and his arms, which had slackened a fraction, tightened again. He opened his eyes, but in the dimness she couldn't see his expression. "Are you cramped?" he asked her.

Triss shook her head, then laid it against his shoulder, warm and smooth and slightly damp with sweat.

After a while Steve shifted, and hooked a hand under one of her thighs, altering her position so that she sat sideways on his knee, one arm still loosely about his neck.

He stroked her thigh and she closed her eyes, lazily enjoying the sensation of his roughened palm on her skin. When he took his hand away she was acutely, stupidly disappointed, but then she felt it slip under the unbuttoned edges of her nightshirt, and when it settled on her breast she gave a sigh of sheer contentment.

She must have drifted into a doze, wakening when Steve said in her ear, "Triss, we have to go. It's nearly dawn."

For a moment she thought she must have dreamed it all, but the strong arms that held her, the solid body so close to hers, were real and substantial. She blinked, then felt the light touch of Steve's lips on hers, lingering before he said again, "We have to go, Triss."

"Yes," she said, hastily moving out of his embrace. They risked being found in a compromising situation, and they'd never hear the end of it from the boys. It could undermine their authority.

Neither of them spoke on the way back to the house. Steve took her to the back door and kissed her hard and quickly. "We'll talk later," he promised, turning toward the annex a few yards away.

The warm indoor atmosphere seemed to curl about her like smoke. She listened for a minute and heard no sound before stealthily making her way up the stairs and back to her own bedroom.

She seemed to be floating in some other world, as though nothing was quite real. The sheets were cold when she climbed between them. Images danced before her closed lids—unbelievable images of herself locked in Steve's arms, of his dark head cradled against her breasts, of her legs tightly wound about his waist.

Never in her life had she so abandoned herself to a man—to the dictates of desire. She hadn't ever thought she was capable of it. That Steve of all people could evoke such passion was unbelievable.

In the cruel light of day it was still unbelievable. Woken by her alarm clock, she killed it and sat up, and the first thing that hit her eye was the picture of Magnus she kept on the bedside table.

Guilt hit her like a blow to the stomach.

What *had* she been thinking of? Nothing but her own pleasure—and her lover's.

Punishing herself under an icy shower, she shivered uncontrollably. How was she going to face him this morning? Or anybody? Illogically she felt that what they had done must be visible to the world.

Crazy, she told herself as she dressed. No one would know—and no one need ever know.

In the dining room she refrained from looking at Steve, choosing to sit at another table and leaving early after breakfast to shut herself in her study.

Of course she knew he wouldn't let things lie. When the house was quiet, all the students in their classes, he tapped on the door and she looked up defensively, her hand tightening about the brass paper knife she was using to slit open an envelope.

He closed the door behind him and his eyes noted

the knife. "You're not planning to use that on me, I hope?"

She laid it down on the desk. "What do you want?"

A faint grin curved his mouth, laughter lurking in his eyes. "I'll give you three guesses."

He moved purposefully toward her, and without thinking Triss shot from her chair and blindly turned from him to stare sightlessly through the window behind her desk, her arms automatically folding about her torso.

Steve must have halted at that. "What's the matter, Triss?"

She took a deep breath before turning to face him, not moving from the window. He was beside the desk, his eyes watchful and probing. She met them with an effort. "I know we can't ignore what happened last night—this morning. We'll just have to be sure it doesn't happen again."

For a moment she wondered if he'd heard. His eyes remained fixed on her, and his face was expressionless. Then his nostrils flared as he pulled in a breath. "Why?"

Triss gestured helplessly. "Isn't it obvious?"

His voice hardened. "As a matter of fact, no. I must be thick. Would you care to explain?"

"I'm Magnus's wife—"

"Widow," he corrected harshly, making her flinch. His mouth clamped so that the skin around it turned white, and a smoldering light entered his eyes. "I'm sorry if that's too blunt for you. But you have to face the fact."

"It's only a matter of a few months!"

"What difference does that make? You're not planning to live like a nun for the rest of your life, are you?''

She had thought she probably would, but Steve had changed all that. ''It's too soon.''

''You didn't think so up there on the hill in the moonlight.''

''I wasn't thinking at all then!'' she snapped, fury with herself translating to fury with him. ''Neither of us was.''

''Speak for yourself! If I'd been incapable of logical thought I'd have stripped us both right there and then and taken you fully, no holds barred and no damned barriers between us. And don't think I didn't want to.''

The explicit, erotic picture he had drawn in her mind took her breath.

''I still want to,'' he said. ''And you can't pretend you don't want it, too.''

Oh, she did, with a fierceness that was almost frightening. Secretly her nails dug into her palms as she fought to make her brain function. ''That's just sex,'' she said.

Mimicking her stance, he folded his arms, rocking on his heels. ''Just sex?'' he echoed thoughtfully. ''Sex is a pretty important human function, sweetie. The continuation of the species depends on it.''

''You weren't planning on continuing the species last night.''

He laughed. ''True. Starting a family together might be a bit premature.''

Triss was visited by an unexpected vision of a dark-haired, gray-eyed child—a solemn little boy just as Steve might have been. A strange emotion compounded of tenderness and longing momentarily stopped her throat. Her voice turned husky. "You must see how impossible it is."

"What's impossible?"

"This…us!"

"Are you afraid of what people will say? I'm not Magnus's son, you know." Steve paused. "If you're thinking you should be in ritual mourning for the conventional year or whatever it is, I don't see the sense of it. Most people will realize you can't put a time frame on the grieving process. It's purely personal."

"Yes, it is. And that's one reason I don't intend to rush into an affair with you."

Impatiently he said, "I don't follow."

"I was married to Magnus for six years. Do you really think I can get over losing him in six months? This…thing may be just a phase." It was so new and unexpected, surely a spurious emotion that couldn't last? "Until very recently we didn't even like each other."

"Not liking you never stopped me from wanting you," Steve told her bluntly. "From the first moment I set eyes on you. As long as I could believe you were a manipulative, deceitful gold digger I could just manage to keep my hands off you. Now—" he shrugged "—I can't."

Triss experienced an extraordinary shift of perspective. "The first moment?" she echoed. *Years,* he'd said last night. She'd thought—as long as she could think at all—that he was exaggerating, using an extravagant superlative in the heat of passion.

He gave her a grim smile. "When you walked in the day you arrived with Magnus. I'd been expecting him of course, and he'd said he was bringing a surprise. Some new piece of equipment for the House, I'd thought, or a famous guest. I was playing an audiotape in the book room and hadn't heard the van arrive. You appeared in the doorway and I didn't know where you'd come from, or have the faintest clue who you were."

"Magnus told me to go in. He was right behind me. I think he wanted to see your reaction."

"In that first second I felt as though I'd been hit in the guts—I couldn't breathe, couldn't think."

Triss's eyes widened, her mouth parting in astonishment.

"You were simply the loveliest thing I'd ever seen. Even in my teens, when my hormones were totally out of control and unpredictable, I'd never had such a powerful reaction to a woman. You were walking toward me, and I was wondering if I was dreaming, then Magnus appeared and put his arm about your waist." Steve stopped to pull in a harsh breath. "I'd known him for nearly nine years and had never seen him touch a woman like that. And he said, 'Steve, say hello to my new wife.'"

"I was sure you'd taken an instant dislike to me."

His mouth took on a grimly ironic twist. "When you smiled at me I wanted to tear his hands off you and grab you for myself. If it had been anyone else but Magnus…hell, I think I might have done it. If not then, later. Do you know what torture I endured in those early days when you kept seeking me out and insisted on talking to me, smiling at me, trying to get me to open up to you?"

"I just wanted to make you feel less…displaced. I was trying to show we could be friends."

Steve shook his head. "I couldn't be your *friend* without wanting much more. Before long I convinced myself you knew how I felt, and enjoyed goading me. Sometimes I was on the brink of blurting out something inane, or even touching you—though I knew I'd never be able to stop at that—and then you'd say that you knew how close Magnus and I were or what hopes he had for me. And I'd grit my teeth and sweat, and hate you for reminding me you belonged to the one man I could never dream of cutting out.''

"Hate me?" Triss whispered. She'd sensed that, known it, but still she was shocked at the interpretation he'd put on her actions. "I only wanted you to know I didn't intend to come between you and Magnus!"

"That's not how it seemed to me at the time."

"I never looked at another man after I met Magnus," Triss said. It was important for Steve to know that, that she wasn't a gold digger or some kind of groupie. "I loved him."

He didn't move, but something in his face altered, his eyelids flickering. His cheeks looked suddenly gaunt and pale.

Had she been cruel, hitting him with that? Remorse twisted in her heart, but he needed to understand. "I know everyone thought, because the age gap was so wide, that I must have had some ulterior motive. His money or his fame. But it wasn't true. Magnus was very special."

Steve nodded jerkily, his face like stone. "He was an extraordinary human being."

"I was enormously privileged to be his wife."

When Magnus proposed, he'd been absurdly diffident about his age and the cruel arthritis that had stiffened his hands and forced him to walk with a cane. "I expect you'll laugh," he'd said, "at an old crock like me."

Of course she hadn't laughed at the idea that this famous, highly respected and good man was asking her to marry him and afraid of being spurned. She admired and respected him tremendously, and surely the warmth that melted her heart at seeing him so humble before her must have been love? And wasn't it love that had made them at ease in each other's company, working harmoniously together at keeping the House running, finding more things in common as they grew to know each other better?

And if so, how could the bewildering emotion that had led to that passionate episode in Steve's arms be the same thing? That was a new experience, both exhilarating and frightening in its intensity, its capacity to threaten her self-control—something that bore no resemblance to the quiet, warm affection that had grown daily deeper between her and Magnus.

This was what falling in love was like, she realized. Something she'd decided would never happen to her, perhaps because she hated uncertainty and craved sureness, serenity, security. She'd seen the chaos "being in love" could cause in other people's lives and feared it for herself, because too often it didn't last. She'd believed what Magnus offered, what he wanted from her, was more mature, more solid. Wasn't it disloyal to his memory to wonder if she'd been shortchanged after all?

Steve gazed down at the floor, his hands shoving into his pockets. When he looked at her again his expression was carefully neutral. "He casts a long shadow."

He wanted to haul her into his arms and kiss her senseless, make her as wild and wanton as she had been last night. He wanted to drive all thought of every

man before him right out of her mind, stop her thinking, stop her caring about anything and anyone but
him.

He'd done it once and he could do it again. The
knowledge stirred his body and shortened his breath.
His hands, hidden inside his pockets, clenched as he
fought down the primitive instinct that made him want
to show her, by force if necessary, how it could be.
Last night she'd been his alone, he would swear to it.
Just as he'd been hers, with no other thought, no other
emotion than their urgent need for each other.

This morning he'd been glad that he'd retained a
tiny measure of self-control. Now he wished he'd
thrown caution to the winds, buried himself deep inside
her, made them truly one flesh, planted his seed in her
so that she'd never be able to forget him.

Just thinking of it made him shake with desire. He
craved her as a desert traveler craved water. And that
fantastic yet unsatisfying episode just a few hours ago
had only made the craving stronger. If half measures
could be that good, what sort of dizzying heights might
they reach when he held her naked in his arms as he
longed to do? As he'd dreamed of doing for so long it
seemed as if she'd always been a part of his life. That
for more than half of it he'd been waiting for her to
appear, and the remainder he'd spent in various kinds
of hell trying to persuade himself he didn't want her.

The pretence was over. He not only wanted her with
a fierce physical ache, he loved her—for her bravery
and steadfastness, her determination, her refusal to be
cowed or daunted, and the unexpected vulnerability
that he'd been so deliberately blind to before.

And she'd knocked him sideways with the simple
statement that she'd loved her husband.

Suddenly she'd become unreachable again. There was no argument he could throw against that wall to breach it. Competing with Magnus had been unthinkable while he lived. Now he was dead, and the unthinkable had become the impossible.

Long after he'd left her standing at the window, with a strange, bleak expression in her eyes, he could clearly hear the echo of her voice saying with utter sincerity, "I loved him."

He didn't want to think about that, never had wanted to. For too long he'd deliberately blanked the idea from his mind. Until Triss had made him face it, a flaming sword between them.

He slammed the door of the music room and went to the keyboard. His fingers raced over the keys, the music tempestuous, abandoned, pouring from his heart to his hands. This was what music was for him—not a public performance, but a private release, an outlet for unwanted emotion.

Concentrate on the sounds, not on the way Triss's mouth had felt under his, how eagerly she'd opened it for him, the thunder in his blood when she'd curled her arms about his neck, the way she'd clung so close and wound her legs about him and angled her body to the imprisoned thrust of his, the way her breath had quickened just before she cried out into his mouth, a cry that held both joy and anguish, exactly mirroring his own feelings at that heady yet unsatisfactory love-making....

Damn! His hands crashed into a series of chords. He leaned forward and buried his head in his hands, breathing hard until the throbbing in his groin at last subsided. He wouldn't take the obvious way out, a solution for adolescents and losers, he'd always thought.

Did she know what she was doing to him? Anger shook him, unfair but cathartic. He had a very tempting picture of marching through the house, finding Triss and without any ceremony picking her up in his arms, carrying her to his bed and throwing her down onto it.

He could see her looking up at him with those wonderful jewel-like eyes, maybe a little fearful, a little guilty, but with desire darkening the centers, watching him as he threw off his clothes and proceeded to tear hers from that beautiful, enticing body, naked at last to him. Her lips parting as he neared them...

And saying, "I loved Magnus."

Steve groaned aloud and thrust his hands into his hair, deliberately tugging until it hurt. *Get a grip, man.* Fantasizing would take him nowhere.

Triss too found it difficult to concentrate. She told herself it was the lack of sleep that had her staring at the large airmail envelope in her hand for several minutes without seeing it. But she couldn't help remembering the way Steve had looked when she told him she had loved her husband. It had obviously been a shock to him.

What on earth had he thought, then?

He'd indicated that his opinion of her character had changed, that he'd realized how wrong he'd been. So why would he retain the idea that her marriage was some kind of sham on her part?

Doing her best to dismiss the whirling thoughts from her mind, she picked up the paper knife and slit the envelope.

Inside were several sheets of paper tucked into a manila folder. She tipped out the folder from the envelope, and a glossy photograph slid from it onto the desk top.

A female face smiled up at her—classically heart-shaped and framed by long, softly curling black hair. Finely arched brows and thick lashes emphasized big dark eyes aimed provocatively at the camera.

Mystified, Triss put aside the photograph and opened the folder. A hand-scrawled note lay on top of the papers beneath.

Dear Steve,
Here's the portfolio you asked for. New Zealand sounds great. Can't wait to see you again, you gorgeous man! We could have some fun!!!
                                        Love, Suzie

A lopsided heart and a series of *X*s followed the signature.

It was so brief she'd skimmed through it before it hit her what she was doing.

She dropped the letter as if it had burned her, and picked up the envelope. The Kurakaha address was neatly typed, and she'd missed the handwritten note on the lower left-hand corner—Attn: Steve.

She looked at the photograph again and went cold, remembering the woman's voice in the background when Steve had called her from L.A. And his voice, lazy and deep, saying, *That's fine, hon, right there. Great.*

Chapter Eleven

Something hot and alien sizzled inside her. Had this Suzie been sharing his bed then? Smiling that sweet, sexy smile while she teased him, aroused him, even while he talked to Triss, thousands of miles away? Or had it been some other "fun" companion?

She wanted to tear the photograph up. Instead she replaced it in the folder with trembling fingers and shoved the whole lot back into the envelope, including the note, and put it aside.

Steve didn't come to lunch. But later in the afternoon Triss heard his unmistakable footsteps in the passageway heading for Magnus's study, which somehow had become Steve's unofficial workroom for Kurakaha business. She picked up the envelope that had been silently leering at her all day, and crossed the short distance to the other room.

The door was ajar and she pushed it wide. "Steve?"

He seemed to have been just standing in the middle

of the room, but at her voice he turned quickly, his eyes searching her face.

Triss held out the envelope to him. Keeping her voice coolly casual, she said, "Sorry, I opened this by mistake."

He took it from her, peeked inside and took out the single-page letter, glanced at it and laughed before tucking it carelessly into his pocket.

Triss's spine stiffened. She turned to leave, but he said, "Don't go, Triss. This is from Susan Stein, the musical director I told you about. She's sent her résumé."

"I don't have time right now."

She'd only taken two steps when he said, "You don't have time, or you can't bear to be in the same room with me?"

Triss spun round. Before she could say anything he asked baldly, "Why? Are you afraid you can't trust yourself? Afraid you might fall off your pedestal of sainted widowhood again and show that you're human? That you're capable of wanting a lesser man than Magnus?"

He couldn't have chosen words more likely to inflame the raw hurt that had been gnawing at her all day. Shaking, she flared at him. "I might have made a mistake last night, but it isn't one I'll ever repeat! Do you really think I'd seriously want a man who... who, as you said yourself, is *lesser* in every way? I suppose women are all the same to you. Sex is something to amuse yourself with when you've nothing better to do. You must have been desperate lately, with no willing, available female around. Well, find yourself another playmate! I'm not available."

She turned her back on his stunned face and was

almost out of the room when his hand on her arm dragged her back and he kicked the door shut with a resounding slam.

"Whoa!" he said grimly, his brows drawn together in a fearsome scowl. "Where the hell did all that come from?"

She tried to pull away but he wouldn't let her, grabbing her other arm too in an implacable grip. "Settle down and tell me what this is really about!"

"I don't have to tell you anything!" She twisted free, but he was between her and the door and she didn't dare take him on.

"Yes, you *bloody* do!" He was angry, too, and the odd thing was she was glad of it. Adrenaline kicked into her veins, and she felt a strange, bitter pleasure.

His head thrust forward, he took a threatening step toward her. "You can't hurl accusations like that and then walk away. Didn't you listen to anything I said to you this morning?"

Triss sucked in a painful breath. She had, and she'd believed him. Until she'd opened that envelope and been consumed by…oh, God! By jealousy. Blind, irrational, corrosive jealousy.

The knowledge was like a blow in her midriff. She felt the blood leaving her cheeks, making her dizzy. "I…" she stammered. "How can I believe you when I know you've been with other women? You might have said the same things to them."

Apparently completely nonplussed, he raised a hand and thrust it through his hair. *"You were married to Magnus,"* he reminded her through gritted teeth. "What was I supposed to do? Of course there were other women—not many, but I was trying my damnedest to forget you, to find someone who made me feel the same way. And no one did. *No one!*"

She trembled at the note of angry despair in his voice. "Not Suzie?" she said foolishly, and immediately bit her lip.

"Suzie?" He looked bewildered.

Triss couldn't help a glance at the envelope he'd dropped when he grabbed her. "I told you," she said, "I opened it. I didn't mean to but I hadn't realized it was for you. I read her note."

"So?" he said as if it meant nothing. He fished the paper from his pocket and shook it out, frowning over it for a moment, then looked up. "You took this seriously?" His tone was incredulous. "Suzie's…a friend. A good friend. So is the man she lives with—the man she's madly in love with. This is—" he waved the note "—just the way she is. Extravagant, teasing. Everybody loves her, including me. But I'm not in love with her and never was, never will be." He crumpled the note carelessly in his hand and tossed it in the general direction of the wastebasket. His eyes narrowed as they refocused on Triss. "You were jealous," he said softly.

No use denying it. She'd betrayed herself too thoroughly for that. "She's beautiful."

Steve gave a shrug that said clearly, So what?

"Was the girl you had with you in your hotel when you phoned me as lovely as that?" Triss asked. She'd already burned several boats and could hardly make this worse.

"What girl?" Steve said blankly.

"You can't have forgotten—unless there've been so many that you've lost track."

He began to look grim again. "Do you want an exact count?"

''No,'' she said hastily, already regretting she'd mentioned this at all. ''It doesn't matter—forget it.'' Boldly she made to pass him, but he caught her arm, stopping her. ''There was no girl there.''

''I heard her.''

''No.'' He shook his head again, seeming baffled.

''It doesn't matter,'' she repeated. ''It's none of my business, after all.''

''Yes it is,'' he insisted, dropping his hand from her arm and standing in front of her again. ''I never phoned you from my hotel.''

''From her place, then.'' Inwardly she winced. That seemed even worse. ''Wherever—she was there! You were talking to her.''

''Talking to her? Saying what?''

''I don't remember.'' The heat rising in her cheeks belied her. Every word was burned in her brain. ''You called her 'honey'.''

The frown between his brows lightened. ''I was at the office,'' he said flatly. ''And back in L.A. mode. It's a thing there—everyone's honey or sweetie or darling.''

He scowled down at her, then after a moment began to laugh, making her want to hit him. She stepped back, glaring.

''A secretary brought me coffee,'' he told her, sobering. ''I remember that now. I guess I thanked her.''

The picture she'd formed had been in the back of her mind for so long she had trouble redrawing it. She'd assumed a hotel room, knowing there was a time difference between Los Angeles and New Zealand, but not pausing to calculate just what it was.

He'd been working, and someone had brought him coffee. Relentlessly her mind filled in the blanks.

That's fine, hon, right there. Great.

Coffee.

"I'm sorry." She was utterly mortified.

"Don't be." He was sober now. "I love it that you were jealous. It must mean something, Triss. You cared."

The way he said it was almost an accusation.

Triss bit down on her lip. "It was purely sexual," she said huskily, a last-ditch, feeble defense.

His eyes went darker and a muscle twitched in his cheek. "I'll settle for that."

Her heartbeat increased. She could scarcely breathe. This was insane, she knew it, and yet she felt the inexorable tug of his sexuality, a siren call to her body that she could no longer ignore.

Forcing her brain to assert itself, she said, "We can't, Steve. We can't have an affair. The boys—it wouldn't be long before they found out." She pictured herself and Steve sneaking into each other's quarters after dark and leaving before dawn, snatching at precarious moments of privacy, possibly being discovered in some intimate embrace.

"I don't care who knows," Steve said. "They're not children. If we're open with them, they'll accept it."

They might, but more likely they'd see an opportunity for sly remarks and sniggering speculation. Or even moral outrage—teenagers, she'd discovered, had remarkably rigid standards for their elders. "What do you plan to do?" she asked. "Make an announcement that we're sleeping together? They'd feel I was betraying Magnus." And so would she. Indulging in an affair under the roof she'd shared with him—there were too many issues, too many risks to the stability of the House and its inmates.

She could see Steve meant to argue, then his teeth snapped shut. He'd seen the logic of her argument and had no answer.

Triss felt his frustration—a frustration she shared. "It will never work."

"It would if we were married."

Her mouth opened but no sound emerged. For the second time in minutes she couldn't breathe. "What?" she finally managed.

"They'd accept that," Steve urged. "Oh, there'd be some disapproval, maybe, because of the short time. But we'd announce it and—" he grinned faintly "—for most of them marriage precludes the idea of unbridled sex. It's an institution for old folks, highly respectable. They'll probably think we're just tidying up the trustee business. So…will you marry me, Triss?"

Stunned, Triss took a couple of seconds to assimilate what he was saying—suggesting. "We can't get married just to…to legitimize having sex!"

His eyebrows quirked up. "Isn't that what it's all about?"

"No! It's about commitment and affection and respect…it's about loving each other. For life."

The hint of humor disappeared, his lips coming together as he gave her a long, intense look. "I love you," he said steadily. "And you want me. It's a start."

Love? He *loved* her? "I…I don't know what to say." She felt dizzy, disoriented.

"Say yes." He took a step toward her and cupped her face in his hands. His eyes were piercing, intent, commanding. "Just say yes."

He kissed her unresisting mouth, at first gently, then

with increasing demand, at last drawing a response from her that seemed to rise from her very soul. The room spun and she had to clutch at him to steady herself. His hands moved to her waist, tugged her almost violently to him, and his thumbs found her rib cage, roughly caressing the rising curve of bone.

Dimly she felt this wasn't fair. He was deliberately confusing the issue, using his sexual power over her to coerce her assent. With reluctant determination she pushed herself away and stood confronting him, surprised that he'd let her do it so easily.

He was breathing fast, his hands hanging at his sides. She put hers to her hot face and then dropped them. His eyes held her gaze, the dark centers nearly obliterating the gray irises. "Say it, Triss," he commanded, his voice deep and grating. "You won't regret it, I swear. Say yes, darling."

The endearment melted some core of resistance. She felt her heart swell and somersault in the most extraordinary way. Why deny him—why deny herself, when every nerve was screaming at her to end the sweet agony of wanting him and not having him?

Marriage wouldn't solve every problem, but what did she have to lose?

This was a rational decision, she told herself. Steve wasn't holding her anymore; she was in control of her senses again. "All right," she heard herself say. "Yes."

Steve closed his eyes for a moment. She thought he swayed a little on his feet. "Thank God," he breathed.

Triss was feeling light-headed now, scarcely believing she'd said it, but there was no going back.

She expected to be swept into his arms again, but once more Steve surprised her. He held out his hands, and when she put hers hesitantly into them he raised them one by one to his mouth and kissed them, then simply stood holding them and staring at her with an almost bemused expression. "I never thought this would happen," he confessed.

"Neither did I."

He looked down at their joined hands, then lifted the left one, staring at the gold band that circled the third finger. Triss made to withdraw, but his grip tightened, then he released her right hand and eased off the ring. He turned her palm up, and pressed a kiss into the shallow hollow. Then he placed the ring in it and folded her fingers over it. "Put it away," he said. He turned her closed fist again and kissed the faint mark the ring had left, before letting her go.

Within days Steve had obtained a marriage license and Triss's consent to a registry office wedding. "Unless you want a church and a minister?" he said. "I expect we could find someone at short notice."

Triss shook her head. Magnus had been a skeptic and in recent years she hadn't attended regularly. A church wedding would have seemed hypocritical.

"I thought we'd have some alterations done to the annex," Steve said. "I've asked an architect to draw up some preliminary sketches."

"Already?"

"It doesn't commit us to anything. I don't want to live in the flat, Triss."

Understandably. But everything about Kurakaha was permeated with its founder's influence. A tremor of uncertainty fluttered in her midriff. "We can't escape Magnus's memory," she warned.

"I know that," Steve said shortly. "But I'm not going to make love to you in his bed."

The carpenters were at work on the alterations even before the wedding. She loved the plan for a larger kitchen area, a refurbished bathroom and an extension to the bedroom opening into a private courtyard. And when she queried the expense Steve said, "I'm paying for it. Call it a wedding present."

They were married on a Friday morning two weeks later, with only Zed and Hana and their children as witnesses, while the students were in classes with their tutors.

When the boys trooped into the dining room for lunch a special feast had been laid out for them, and Hana had placed a large square white-iced cake, trimmed with silver bells and love knots, before Triss and Steve.

Zed made a speech and broke the news. Following a moment of stunned silence, a chorus of cheers and whistles and applause broke out, and Triss almost cried with relief.

Steve's hand closed about hers as Zed proposed a toast to them, and the boys rose to the occasion, solemnly lifting glasses of the strictly limited amount of sparkling wine Steve had provided.

He thanked them briefly and graciously, and after they'd gone back to their classrooms he and Triss discreetly drove off for a weekend at a beach resort, leaving Zed and Hana in charge.

Steve had booked them into a seafront unit at a five-star motel with its own restaurant. He carried in their two overnight bags and placed them on a luggage rack inside the door, then looked at the king-size bed that occupied pride of place in the room.

Triss averted her eyes and slipped off her shoulder bag to place it on the dressing table.

Steve's arms came about her from behind, his lips nuzzling the curve between her neck and shoulder. She shivered with a combination of anticipation and nervousness. "I need the bathroom," she said in strangled tones.

His hands slid possessively to her hips before he stepped back, allowing her to pass him.

This was silly, she told herself a few minutes later, splashing cold water over her face before burying it in a towel. She *wanted* to have sex with Steve. To put it in brutally honest terms, it was why she'd married him. So why was she dithering about like some nineteenth-century bride?

When she emerged Steve was lying on the bed with his hands behind his head. His feet were bare but otherwise he was fully dressed. Through the window she could see the ocean, blue and limitless, dancing with white wavelets and glancing shafts of sunlight.

He turned his head to look at her. Triss hesitated, then carefully shut the bathroom door behind her.

Steve seemed to be assessing her. He altered his position, propping himself on one elbow. "Take off your shoes," he said.

Her heart gave a hard thump. "What?" she faintly. Her shoes, and then what? Was he planning to watch her strip for him? A curious sensation curled inside her, part indignation and part excitement.

"Take off your shoes," Steve repeated. He sat up, swinging his feet to the floor. "We'll go for a walk on the beach—unless you'd prefer to stay here and do something else?" His brows lifted suggestively.

Triss said hastily, "A walk sounds good."

"Funny, that's what I thought you'd say." He stood up as she slipped out of her high-heeled pumps. His hand reached up and he tucked a strand of hair behind her ear. "What are you scared of?" he asked softly.

"I'm not scared!"

He made a disbelieving grimace. "Okay, if you say so." Possessing himself of her hand, he drew her toward the door leading to a lawn that sloped gently down to the sand. "Come on, let's walk."

They walked, and he didn't let go of her hand. The beach was long and wide and there were few other people there. They climbed a narrow path up a headland at the end of it, between rattling flax and wind-bowed manuka, and stood looking at the pale stretch of sand and the sun-kissed waves that smoothed it.

Steve found a softly grassed hollow at the foot of an old twisted puriri, and settled himself behind her, cradling her between his thighs, his arms about her waist. "Relax," he murmured. "All I want is to hold you."

She let her head rest against him, and gradually the tension eased from her. Below them a school of fish swirled in the water, clearly visible. A yellow-beaked gannet circled above and then tucked its wings close and dived, scattering the school and emerging with a flapping fish held fast, which it quickly swallowed.

Triss shivered. "Poor fish."

"Gannets have to eat. Which reminds me, are you hungry?"

"Not yet. Are you?"

Silent laughter shook his chest. She felt it against her back. "There's an obvious answer to that."

Triss ducked her head, and he put his lips to her exposed nape, giving her a tiny nip with his teeth.

Before she could react he'd moved his mouth away. "But I can wait," he said.

When her heart had stopped pounding and she hoped her voice was steady, she said, "Let's go back."

She thought he might not have heard because it seemed an age before he answered, "Sure?"

"I'm sure." There was no reason to wait. She'd married him, for better or worse. And whatever happened afterward she was very sure that the first time they really made love was definitely going to be for the better.

She wasn't wrong. They didn't hurry, strolling along the beach as if they had all the time in the world, with Steve's arm hooked about her shoulder, seemingly casual. But the thumb that absently caressed her bare shoulder sent shivers of anticipation running along all her nerve ends, and when she stooped to pick up a perfect half-moon shell with delicate pink edging, and glanced at him as she straightened, his eyes were narrowed, glittering slits in a taut face.

As he closed the door of the unit she said breathlessly, "I'm all sandy. I should wash my feet in the shower."

She hurried, running the shower over her feet one by one, then grabbed a towel and went back to the bedroom.

Steve had closed the curtains and stripped off his shirt. He looked magnificent. The man had a body to die for—no wonder she was lusting after it.

He gave her a crooked grin and headed for the bathroom. "I won't be long," he promised, sending her a lingering glance, full of unspoken promises.

Triss toweled her feet dry, sitting on the edge of the bed. She opened her overnight bag and hauled out some of the few clothes she'd brought, digging for her hairbrush.

She never had cut her hair, since the day Steve had told her it was beautiful. Lately she'd been twisting a hair tie about it in the daytime, leaving it loose at night. Today she'd let it free, falling about her shoulders, and now it felt windblown and tangled.

In the bathroom the shower was running. Not with cold water, she assumed, smiling to herself, her cheeks warm.

She found the brush and smoothed the tangles out to a soft shine, then hung some clothes in the wardrobe. The shower stopped, and moments later Steve appeared, a white towel loosely tucked about his waist. He looked at her standing by the wardrobe, crossed to the bed and pulled away the covers, exposing the bottom sheet.

Then he strolled toward Triss, holding her eyes with his. Without a word he gently turned her, opened the zip of her dress, and pushed the straps down her arms so that the garment fell, pooling at her feet.

''Look at me, Triss,'' he said very quietly.

She turned slowly, expecting him to be making a greedy survey of her body, clad now only in a lacy bra and matching bikini briefs, hardly any covering at all.

Instead he gazed into her eyes, his own fathomless and unreadable. He took a deep breath into his chest, and his arms slid about her shoulders and under her knees. He picked her up and carried her to the bed.

She had not anticipated gentleness or patience, but he gave her both. He touched her face with his hands so lightly she scarcely felt it, but a feathery sensation ran along her nerves to the pit of her stomach. He kissed her shoulders, her wrists, her feet. She hadn't known that the arch of her instep was an erogenous zone, or the inside of her knee.

And she hadn't known that her fingers making tiny circles around a man's nipples, or her mouth on the taut skin of his midriff, could make him groan with pleasure and stretch his big body like a huge, sleek cat, inviting her to explore further.

But when she did, he growled, "No, not there…not yet." He flipped her onto her stomach and undid her bra, and began stroking her, finding every curve and hollow along the way from her neck to the base of her spine. And then he started from her toes and stroked her legs until she was nearly screaming with delicious tension.

When his hands tugged at her panties she almost sobbed with relief. She lifted herself, helping, and made to turn, but his hands on her thighs stopped her.

"What are you doing?" she asked him.

"Admiring the view." His hands moved lazily over the curves he'd uncovered. It was wonderful, lovely, but after a minute she turned over, grumbling, "It's all very well for you. I can't see a thing."

Steve laughed. "So what do you want to do about it?" he taunted her.

The towel had slipped to his hips. She reached out and tugged, and it fell away.

Her tongue stole between her parted lips. Heavy-lidded, she lifted her eyes to his face. "Well!" she said inadequately.

Steve smiled and, leaning forward, removed her bra completely, threw it on the floor, then sat back on his haunches. "And this view is even better," he told her huskily. He trailed one finger from the hollow at the base of her throat, down over her breasts, taking a short detour there, and pausing for a second at her navel. Her breathing quickened, and when he looked into her eyes, asking a silent question, she knew he'd seen the answer. But she'd had enough teasing, enough foreplay. "I want you," she whispered. "I want *that*." Her gaze dropped momentarily, and as his finger touched the tiny nub of desire he'd been heading for, she parted her legs and closed her eyes, her breath hissing between her teeth, her whole body clenching.

His answer was fast and silent. There was a second of hiatus, then his solid, warm body covered her, his arms cradling her, his breath mingled with hers as their mouths met, and when he entered he was smooth and hot and heavenly.

He loved her, loved her with deep, hard thrusts of his body, mimicked by the movements of his tongue in her mouth, and with his hands, one cradling her breast, the other supporting her head. He loved her with every part of his body, tenderly and then with increasing fierceness, until shuddering gasps shook him, just before she was taken over by a wave of such intense pleasure that she thought she could die of it. She went rigid in his arms, poised on the brink of another wave, then limp as it took her even higher, and was dimly conscious of Steve's hands holding her safe, of his voice in her ear telling her she was wonderful, beautiful, fantastic, urging her on, and on.

Chapter Twelve

When the cataclysm had subsided to a series of tiny aftershocks and she lay utterly spent in his arms, he turned them both, still locked together, and she collapsed against him, her head tucked under his chin, while he caressed her back.

"That was unbelievable," Steve murmured.

Silently, stunned, Triss echoed the sentiment. She'd thought she knew about sex, but never had it been like this.

Surely it could never be like that again. Yet minutes later she realized that although she'd been sure she was exhausted, her body didn't agree.

Again they climaxed together, and it was different but no less shattering.

Way past dark when they showered and dressed and went to the restaurant for dinner.

For three days nothing existed but their absorption in each other. They swam, and walked on the beach, ate when they felt like it, made love in a secluded nook they discovered among the trees above the sand and once after dark on a blanket spread on the cool sand itself. And more times than they could count in the big bed in their room, at any time of the day or night.

They had to return to Kurakaha and normality of course. They consulted with accountants and a share broker and, with the proviso that no investment was to directly fly in the face of Magnus's principles, Triss allowed them to redistribute his stocks and shares.

An advisory committee of Kurakaha old boys was set up to help determine future policy. Donations from past students and others to the memorial fund they'd set up allowed the trust to be resettled on a sound footing.

By unspoken agreement they kept business separate from their marriage. During the day they had to resist the temptation to touch in public in case their mutual hunger was too obvious. But after dark they allowed their passion free rein.

It couldn't last, Triss told herself. And yet six months later nothing had changed. Sexually they were perfectly attuned. More often than not they reached the peak together, and then they developed a torturous refinement, making it a lovers' game to see who could drive the other over the edge first. But the laggard was never far behind, because watching each other was an incitement.

One night they took a blanket and pillows and crept out of the house to the grotto on the hill and made love in the moonlight. It was magical, mysterious and wonderful, being naked and together under the stars, and afterward Steve wrapped them both in the blanket and propped the pillows against the stone wall and leaned back with Triss in his arms, her shoulder resting on his bare chest, his cheek against her hair.

The trees whispered and trembled, and far away in the distance a moving light indicated the path of the motorway, followed moments later by another.

Triss said, "I used to sit up here sometimes and wish I could go far, far away. At least for a while."

"Used to?"

Surprise held her still. She hadn't felt that way for months—since she'd married him, in fact.

Steve's chest rose and fell with a deeper breath. "We can, you know..."

"The House—"

"...live somewhere else—get in a competent paid administrator, even a couple."

"But..." Such a radical plan had never occurred to her.

"We could make ourselves a home in Auckland—or anywhere. Even in L.A. Just you and me."

Surely he couldn't be serious.

Both tempted and terrified, Triss burst out, "Magnus would never have allowed—"

She broke off with a gasp as Steve twisted inside the blanket and gripped her shoulders, turning her to face him. "Magnus is *dead!* For God's sake, Triss, *let the man go!*"

The tearing pain in his voice stopped the breath in her throat, pierced her heart. "I'm sorry, Steve," she whispered, "but—"

"Think about it!" he said fiercely. His fingers dug into her flesh. The blanket slipped, and cool night air shivered along her shoulders. "It's possible, Triss! All we've done over the past year has made it possible. We don't have to be tied forever to Kurakaha, living in Magnus's shadow. *Please,* darling! Give our marriage a chance.''

The plea shook her to the core. She'd been fooling herself that Steve was satisfied with sex. That *she* was. Their physical relationship was so good, so mindblowing, that she'd been able to blot everything else out each time they came together, and kept herself too busy with Kurakaha business the rest of the time to think about anything else.

Now Steve was asking her to think, to make a drastic decision.

''We can spend time here,'' he said. ''As much as it needs. We could even live in the annex for part of each year. But first we need to get away from here, at least for a while—we never even had a proper honeymoon.''

It was true. They'd snatched a few days here, a weekend there. Never long enough.

Another headlight sped along the distant road, cutting across the dark. Triss felt a sudden rush of a strange, heady feeling. Maybe it was freedom.

''You're right,'' she said wonderingly, hearing her voice remotely as if it were someone else's, coming from afar. ''Of course we could live somewhere else. We could!''

The breath escaped from his body. ''Thank you,'' he said, his hands sliding to her waist, making the blanket slip farther. ''Thank you, Triss.''

The blanket fell, and received them as he bore her to the ground. There was a new quality in the way he made love to her, touching her shoulders, breasts, thighs, kissing them. Or perhaps the difference was in her—a new peace of heart, a kind of relaxed tranquility that gradually changed to heated, passionate response.

For the first time Steve didn't stop to place a gossamer barrier between them, only looking down at her moonlit face for a poised moment, silently asking her agreement. She gave it with a tiny nod, and pulled his head down to feel his mouth on hers as he glided sweetly and surely into the satiny depths of her womanhood.

Two months later they were walking on a wide, windy beach, their arms about each other.

Triss paused to gather a perfect spiral shell, rubbing sand from its golden curves, and Steve picked up a flat stone and hurled it over an incoming crest to the calm water where it skipped five times before sinking.

He turned with a triumphant grin to Triss, who laughed at him. "Practice makes perfect," she teased. "You've only been trying for a week."

"And I've got another week to keep trying," he said, his arm hooking about her waist again. "Maybe I can better my record."

She slanted a teasing glance at him. "I doubt that."

Steve's answering grin was wicked. "Try me."

Triss shook her head, laughing again. "Even you must have limits, Superman."

Their bare feet splashed through the last inch of an incoming wave. There was no one else within sight, the wide dark sands smooth under the looming cliffs, rippled into ridges where the waves had shaped them. "It was clever of you to find this beach," she told him. "Sometimes I think it's another dream."

"This," he said, "is not a dream." He dropped a quick kiss on her mouth. "It wasn't all that hard when I knew where you'd lived. I'd like to make all your dreams come true, Triss."

"You've made a good start," she said softly. "This holiday—our home." They were building one, a private place amid native bush and overlooking a peaceful estuary. "But I don't need dreams now."

Dreams, longings for past happiness, for lost childhoods, were for people whose reality in the here and now was less than perfect. Who had no confidence in the future. "I'm looking forward to seeing Los Angeles." Because he was due to spend a month or two there, and she'd agreed this time to accompany him. By the time they returned their house would be ready to move into. Their shared future a solid reality.

"Steve," she said, trying to sound casual, "there's something else."

"What?" He turned his head to kiss her hair.

"I think I'm pregnant."

Steve abruptly stopped walking. His hands dropped from her and he stood motionless.

"Are you surprised?" she asked him. "It isn't as though we haven't been inviting it."

"I...wasn't sure," he said hoarsely, "if you wanted it or...you knew it couldn't happen."

Triss blinked. He'd thought she might be sterile?

Of course, after being married to Magnus for six years with no children...

But he'd never asked. And she'd never told him that Magnus had felt he was too old to start a family, that at the time it hadn't mattered. She liked children but had not believed herself to be particularly maternal. Not then.

She hadn't thought she was particularly sexual either. Steve had taught her how wrong she'd been about that. "I wouldn't have married you," she said, "if I'd thought I could never have your child. Not without telling you.''

''It wouldn't have mattered,'' he said. ''Are you happy?''

''Happier than I've ever been in my life,'' she said, with utter certainty. Steve had found the empty, aching place in her heart that even Magnus had been unable to penetrate. With him she felt fulfilled, whole and loved, with nothing missing from her life. So happy she could hardly contain it.

His eyes queried that, and for a moment she glimpsed the unloved, insecure child he had once been. ''It's true,'' she said. ''With Magnus—''

She saw the shutters descend behind his eyes, his shoulders stiffen. Even his face tautened in rejection.

''Oh, don't!'' She put a hand on his arm, and when he would have instinctively jerked away she closed her fingers and held on. ''I need to say this, Steve.'' Otherwise the shadow would always lie between them. ''You know how Magnus was, how he made people admire him, love him, without even trying.''

''He tried with you.''

''I suppose.'' She hesitated. ''Do you know, I don't think he even noticed how I looked? But he did like me, and…I think he kind of liked the *idea* of me…of a young woman making other men his age envy him. Magnus wasn't entirely devoid of vanity. But if he hadn't admired my office skills, he'd probably not have asked me to marry him.''

''Are you saying it wasn't love?''

''He was fond of me. And I did love him…'' She saw the tremor that he tried to hide with a scowl, and reached up with her free hand to smooth away the deep grooves under her finger. ''…only not like this. I hate to bow to the old cliché, but I guess he was the obvious, classic father figure—older, wiser, stable. What I felt for him was genuine, but it wasn't at all the way I love you. With all my heart and soul, mind and body.''

He grabbed her wrist and pulled her hand away, but held it in a hard grip. "What?'' he said hoarsely, as if unable to believe his ears.

"I love you.'' She looked into his eyes, willing him to listen. The knowledge had dawned on her slowly, and she couldn't have told him when she had begun to love him with that bone-deep, steadfast trueness that was more than sex and more than friendship but melded both within its crucible. "I said once you were a lesser man. That was cruel and untrue. You're not perfect—I know that. It's just as well, because neither am I. And Magnus wasn't either. He was just a man, after all. A man I once loved in a different way…but so did you. A part of our past. *You* are my future, you and our baby. And I'm yours.''

"Mine?''

"Always.'' She lifted the hand he still held and turned it to press her lips to his knuckles, then laid her cheek against them. "I'm so sorry I hurt you.'' Because she knew she had, refusing to acknowledge his feelings for her, brushing aside his declaration of love when he'd asked her to marry him. "I'll make it up to you, I promise.'' There was no need to feel guilty because Steve stirred depths of emotion that Magnus had never asked for and that she hadn't known she possessed.

"You already have.'' He pulled her close, chest to chest, cheek to cheek. "You married me. It was enough. But this…this is more than I ever hoped for.''

"Oh, Steve." He'd asked for so little, and given her so much. His unconditional love, her freedom. His child. Already she felt a fierce protectiveness, a melting tenderness for the unseen, scarcely recognized new life within her. Their baby. Unbelievable that once she'd thought motherhood unimportant.

A rogue wave broke about their knees, and cold salt spray mingled with hot tears on her cheeks.

"You're crying!" Steve took her face between his big hands, wiping at the moisture with his thumbs. "Why?"

Triss gave a shaky laugh. "Expectant mothers get emotional," she said.

Steve looked into her eyes and remembered that once he'd seen steel in them. Now they were brilliant and blurry with tears, and looked at him with love.

He kissed the tears away, and kissed her mouth, which flowered eagerly under his. Another wave buffeted them and they scarcely noticed, but after a while he lifted her in his arms and carried her farther up the sand. "I want to make love to you," he said deeply.

Triss wanted it, too. "Put me down," she said. "You can't carry me all the way to the house."

"Is that a challenge?" he growled. But already his feet were sinking into the dry sand, his breathing heavier.

She gave a soft gurgle of laughter. "I don't want you exhausted before we get there."

He grinned and put her down. "No chance."

"Come on, then." She took his hand and walked backward, leading him up the slope. "See if you can better your record."

A long time later, lying on the bed in happy exhaustion, watching the sun sink in fiery glory across the water, she conceded that he had.

* * * * *

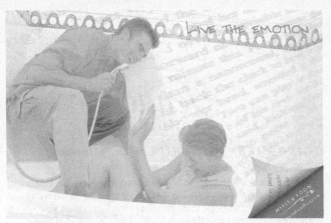

LIVE THE EMOTION

Modern
romance™

...international affairs
– seduction and
passion guaranteed

Medical
romance™

...pulse-raising
romance – heart-
racing medical drama

Tender
romance™

...sparkling, emotional,
feel-good romance

Sensual
romance™

...teasing, tempting,
provocatively playful

Historical
romance™

...rich, vivid and
passionate

Blaze™

...scorching hot
sexy reads

27 new titles every month.

Live the emotion

MILLS & BOON®

MB5

MILLS & BOON®

Live the emotion

Tender
romance™

GINO'S ARRANGED BRIDE by Lucy Gordon

(The Italian Brothers)

All Laura's little girl wants is a daddy to love her. So Laura marries Italian Gino Farnese, believing a paper marriage is the best they can hope for. But there are two rules: no sharing a bed and no falling in love. And they're in danger of breaking them both...

A PRETEND ENGAGEMENT by Jessica Steele

Varnie was startled when she found a man in her bedroom – even more that the man was Leon Beaumont, her brother's boss! But her brother's job was at risk if Varnie didn't let Leon stay. It seemed they were stuck with each other – especially when the newspapers annouced their engagement!

HER SPANISH BOSS by Barbara McMahon *(9 to 5)*

When Rachel Goodson starts working for Luis Alvares he's prickly and suspicious. But soon they draw closer and secrets spill out. Luis's heart is still with his late wife, so Rachel is stunned when he wants her to pose as his girlfriend. Luis wants more than just a pretend relationship...

A CONVENIENT GROOM by Darcy Maguire

(The Bridal Business)

When Riana Andrews woke to find an engagement ring on her finger she was more than a little confused! The guy she *thought* had proposed was Joe Henderson, a sexy photographer. He was certainly acting like her fiancé, and she wasn't imagining the tingles she got around him!

On sale 6th August 2004

Available at most branches of WHSmith, Tesco, Martins, Borders, Eason, Sainsbury's and all good paperback bookshops.

MILLS & BOON®

**Volume 2
on sale from
6th August
2004**

Lynne
Graham
International Playboys
*A Savage
Betrayal*

*Available at most branches of WHSmith, Tesco, Martins, Borders,
Eason, Sainsbury's and all good paperback bookshops.*

4 FREE

books and a surprise gift!

We would like to take this opportunity to thank you for reading this Mills & Boon® book by offering you the chance to take FOUR more specially selected titles from the Tender Romance™ series absolutely FREE! We're also making this offer to introduce you to the benefits of the Reader Service™—

- ★ FREE home delivery
- ★ FREE gifts and competitions
- ★ FREE monthly Newsletter
- ★ Exclusive Reader Service offers
- ★ Books available before they're in the shops

Accepting these FREE books and gift places you under no obligation to buy, you may cancel at any time, even after receiving your free shipment. Simply complete your details below and return the entire page to the address below. *You don't even need a stamp!*

YES! Please send me 4 free Tender Romance books and a surprise gift. I understand that unless you hear from me, I will receive 6 superb new titles every month for just £2.69 each, postage and packing free. I am under no obligation to purchase any books and may cancel my subscription at any time. The free books and gift will be mine to keep in any case.

N4ZED

Ms/Mrs/Miss/Mr ....Initials................................

BLOCK CAPITALS PLEASE

Surname ....

Address ....

....

....Postcode................................

Send this whole page to:
UK: FREEPOST CN81, Croydon, CR9 3WZ
EIRE: PO Box 4546, Kilcock, County Kildare (stamp required)